SHORE TO SHORE

TAMSIN HOPKINS

INDEPENDENT INNOVATIVE INTERNATIONAL

Published by Cinnamon Press
Meirion House
Tanygrisiau
Blaenau Ffestiniog
Gwynedd LL41 3SU
www.cinnamonpress.com

The right of Tamsin Hopkins to be identified as author of this work has been asserted by her in accordance with the Copyright, Designs and Patent Act, 1988. © 2016 Tamsin Hopkins
ISBN 978-1-910836-16-3
British Library Cataloguing in Publication Data. A CIP record for this book can be obtained from the British Library.
Designed and typeset in Garamond by Cinnamon Press. Cover design by Adam Craig © Adam Craig.
Cinnamon Press is represented by Inpress and by the Welsh Books Council in Wales.
Printed in Poland

The publisher gratefully acknowledges the support of the Welsh Books Council.

Contents

Hani's Baby　　　　　　　　　　　7
Orphaline　　　　　　　　　　　21
Inundation　　　　　　　　　　42
Cenotes　　　　　　　　　　　66
Joanna Brown　　　　　　　　119
Day of the Dead　　　　　　　139
The Tow Path　　　　　　　　153
Sand Tranny　　　　　　　　　165

for SRBP

SHORE TO SHORE

Hani's Baby

He was in such a hurry to get to Baby Cheeks that dark morning he almost didn't know what he was doing – his fingers were like fat little bananas and it took him what seemed like minutes to clip the safety belt round the overnight bag, he wasn't comfortable touching it and he didn't want to squash what was inside. As he pulled his Fiesta into the parking area, he looked in the rear view mirror and saw his own face, grey in the pre-dawn shadow; he was surprised to realise that he knew exactly what he was doing.

There was always someone at the take-off point. It was a large field, which the company rented but someone would be there who could help him rig and inflate his balloon. Two or three men were praying in a corner. One was boiling water. Hani found a man he knew and looking at his own feet, passed him some folded bank notes. After that, things moved quickly. They spread the pale balloon envelope out on the ground together, the company logo uppermost – a red swirl of letters that made Hani think of a smiling mouth on puffed out cheeks. The attendant brought the air fan whilst Hani attached the burner valves; the propane tanks and the wicker gondola to the balloon skirt and laid the gondola on its side. He sorted through the guy ropes, running his hand over every line. Then he wheeled the fan over to the envelope mouth and partially inflated it whilst the attendant held the crown line for him so he could walk inside the billowing cranial cavity, checking Baby Cheeks over for tears.

Soon the panelled gores plumped up and Baby Cheeks began to roll, giving the attendant some trouble. Hani tested the drop line, which was tethered to a hook in the ground, and then he returned to his Fiesta. He opened the door, holding his breath, half dreading the smell that wasn't there yet. Seeing the bag still on the seat, its sad form, he thought to himself that Ayesha would start to feel better in a few days. She would come to terms with what he had done. Hani gently took up the handles of the overnight bag and returned to Baby Cheeks. If he was going, it had to be now.

Checking the rig again out of habit, Hani fired up the burner; the basket began to right itself as Baby Cheeks lifted from the ground. He jumped into the gondola and uncoupled the drop line, automatically scanning for obstacles as they rose.

Hani held the burner valves open and after a few seconds, they were on their way. Although it was an hour before dawn, several farmers were already working amongst the sugarcane plants. Far away to the left, two massive silhouettes grew out of the darkness, seated pharaohs, patiently waiting to salute the dawn. The Colossi of Memnon. People said that in antiquity one of them used to sing to the dawn, the dew expanded in the sandstone and cracked it or some such phenomenon. The tourists liked that kind of thing but Hani had never heard any statue sing.

As he watched the fields recede, it occurred to him that he had rarely taken Baby Cheeks up for his own pleasure, never before simply for the joy of flight, for the freedom and the silence. It had always been for other people, instructors or tourists, Ayesha, or trips he was bullied into by her brothers. Hani had looked forward to the family occasions at first – the meals, the lifts he was happy to give, the parties and the shopping trips. He had even been glad to join a more religious family. They did everything with such dynamism and he wanted to be part of that. He thought some of that energy might transfer to him and with it perhaps even some of their faith.

Maybe he was a bit slow on the uptake he thought, because it had taken him some time to realise that Ayesha's father was a back slapper who smiled and nodded, but otherwise didn't say or do much. Ayesha's mother organised everything. It hadn't been long before he found the whole experience exhausting. They were always calling him to go with this brother here, take that cousin there, come to this party or that meeting and always there was the mosque, the prayers. God knows he didn't resent the prayers. He just couldn't keep up.

He burned more gas and checked with a gentle nudge of his foot that the overnight bag was safely stowed in a corner of the basket. It was going to be cold up there. He had known from the first cries of the women what he would do. He hadn't told Ayesha. He had kissed her sweating cheek and fled with his burden, leaving her behind.

Hani blasted flame into the mouth of the balloon, needing to get away before anybody else came. Baby Cheeks and he were the first up but the others would be along soon to take advantage of the calm early winds. He inhaled a jagged breath, sniffed and looked around the gondola. They had cleared the fields but now were in wind taking them the wrong way, going east towards the river. The dawn was coming, a thin pink line creeping up out of the far desert horizon, not yet touching the town and river below. Life, rising from the East. A prayer came to his lips although he had missed Fajr. Allah hu akbar – God is great. He took off his glasses and wiped his eyes with a thumb. A little while later, he straightened his jacket, released more flames into the balloon and looked towards the East, beyond Luxor. There was little real wind. Higher up and later in the day the winds would begin to move but now, looking at the horizon, Baby Cheeks appeared to hang in the air for a while. It was an illusion of equilibrium; he knew they were drifting down. Allah the Cherisher. The Sustainer. The Compassionate. The Merciful.

Wanting to see the eastern horizon clearly, Hani opened the burners with a series of sustained blasts, forcing Baby

9

Cheeks to climb and after a while they had risen high enough to see both sides of the river clearly. The Nile was as placid as a lake. No tide, no crocodiles, no flooding. Emasculated. Contained. Kept. The most obvious thing people noticed from the air, the thing which everybody commented on, was the green ribbon that tracked the body of the Nile like a sheath as far as the eye could see. The river's strength still influenced the land surrounding the river-bank, the old floodplain, for about half a kilometre on either bank, which Hani took to be the practicable distance for irrigation. Beyond that, people seemed to give up.

Away to one side on the east was the promenade where Ayesha liked to go with her cousins and sisters in the evenings. They would leave their mother on a bench with her friends. She waited there like a bulbous Nile toad, her skin patterned with age spots, peering through her thick glasses until her daughters came back into focus and collected her, by which time she had usually lost her temper with one or more of the other women sitting nearby. Ayesha was the only one who didn't have a buggy to push along the promenade, a toddler of her own to run after. She told people she had plenty of time for nappies, nieces and nephews were enough, but everyone knew she wanted children. That was why they had got her a husband.

He tried. It was true, everybody had children, sons, daughters, babies everywhere, except Hani and Ayesha. He did his best, he had always thought Ayesha was beautiful. He loved her voice and his breath caught in his throat at the thought of her warm skin and the curve of her breasts. If he was driving or up in the balloon, he would have to fight to keep his mind on what he was doing.

His father-in-law gave him cartons of Marlboro, which piled up in a cupboard because he didn't smoke. The back-slapping and smiling increased. Ayesha's brothers would wink at him, which Hani ignored. He had to perform twice a day, every day. Before work and after work. It wasn't long before Ayesha began to cry after their love-making. She lay with her face turned to the window and didn't wipe the tears away. Then she would get up and turn into something else. It was awful. She'd be screaming at him. They should be a proper family. Why had she not conceived? Why would he not let her have what she needed? What did he do? Did he spend himself on undeserving women so that nothing useful was left for her? Didn't he love her? What more could she do to encourage him? He knew this was intended to goad him, to raise a fiery response. She knew that he didn't go elsewhere for sex. It was only that he was exhausted.

In time, thanks be to God, Ayesha conceived. She settled into a big armchair like a plump duck on a nest and let everybody look after her. She seemed to swell more every day; within a month she had filled the chair. After two months, she was huge, and pale and bored. Hani felt dried out, reduced to a twig, a stick man trying to appease her with extra cushions and custards made from evaporated milk; her mother and sisters were never out of his house but he never quite knew what it was they did. One day when Hani got home, he put his keys in the basket by the door and saw that her chair was empty; it had been covered in towels and Ayesha had moved to the bedroom where he could hear her crying in the dark. They left them alone that time. He held her hand and they prayed quietly.

Six weeks later, her face a grey moon with dark yellow craters under her eyes, Ayesha announced that she was ready to start again. Hani had been dreading this. There had to be a son, Hani had to be a man, so they began their forced morning and evening ritual all over again. It was as if they were on a ghastly journey with no way to change their destination and Hani dreamed he was flying Baby Cheeks and couldn't find a way to let the air out and bring the balloon down. The winking and nudging from Ayesha's brothers and the cigarettes and backslapping from her

11

father started up again but Ayesha's mother paid him no attention whatsoever. Despite Hani's efforts, their situation didn't improve. They saw doctors. Ayesha cried. The pattern of their lives seemed set to continue, struggling to conceive, hope and then misery. She would never give up. He didn't know what to say to her. Then, Allah be praised, they conceived their son. They even dared to talk about names. He was tougher than the others, their son. He hung on for longer.

Hani ran his hands over the padded bumper that covered the edge of the basket, smoothing a bubble with his thumb. Maybe the doctor would have arrived by now. Maybe Ayesha would have to go to hospital. She hadn't the last time, but this baby had got further. She had thought it was going to be okay this time. Last night, that had changed. Their apartment had become hot, noisy, filled with pendulous breasts, bare arms, urgent voices and, strangely, the absence of perfume. Thanks be to God that the women had dealt with everything. He could not have coped.

The living town of Luxor was waking up slowly, lights coming on and the occasional car nosing along. Hotels and casinos dominated the river-front and Hani could also make out the pillared frontage of the rowing club. He had taken some tourists up to see a regatta once. They had looked down at the river and watched the perfectly spaced circles the oars made in the water, skimming across the surface with insectoid precision.

Near the centre of town was the train station with roads radiating away from it, Mostafa Kamel, Television Street, Salah Salem, all running parallel to the Nile until they cleared the grey of the city. Buildings became lower and closer together until, by the time they touched the desert they were little more than piles of breeze-blocks and cardboard. The airport was a geometric scratch in the sand.

Underneath the balloon, flapping with deep, slow beats of its wings, a heron crossed the river from east to west, reflected white on the surface of the water despite the grey light. Small boats were making ready to shuttle tourists across to the coaches that would collect them on the west side and take them to the Valley of the Kings. Hani flared the burner again. The rush of burning propane was the only sound in the predawn calm.

His glasses slipped down his nose again; they were an old pair he kept in the car. He had a pair with elastic around the back, but he must have left them. On the dining table probably; he had been sitting alone at the head of the table for most of the night. He wondered what was going on at home.

Hani had been leaning heavily on the padded rail. He shifted his weight and glanced at the overnight bag. It hadn't moved. They drifted further east, the air current taking Baby Cheeks away from their destination for a while so that they now hung directly above the Nile. For a few minutes they followed the course of the river suspended, encapsulated in a timelessness that belonged to the river itself. The Nile ran through the middle of everything, he thought, which was especially obvious at Luxor. Death, endless graves on the west side. Life on the east. The town, like the people, always divided by something. The new and the old. The desert and the life. The desert did not have to mean death. It could mean a hard existence but a pure one. It could stand for endurance. That's what he'd heard.

Hanging there above the Nile, he was afraid they would be spotted before they got far enough away, so Hani took Baby Cheeks up further, looking for wind that would take them west again. They climbed above the green expanse of flood plain that stretched flat all the way from the river bank until it ran up against the red cliffs at Deir el-Bahari, where the tourists swarmed like flies every day of the year, boiling up the sloped entrance to admire Hatshepsut's red colonnades. At about three thousand feet Hani found a strong current that would take them in the right direction. With a series of blasts on the burner he maintained that height, dipping and lifting again in a succession of vertical zigzags.

Towards his left, to the west of the Nile, the red cliffs were coming into focus although the dawn here lagged behind the light which had reached the town of Luxor, on the east bank. He watched rectangular blocks of shadows form around the temple of Hatshepsut, its long forecourt sweeping regally forwards, its back jammed up hard against the hills. The rest, beyond the cliffs, the Valley of the Kings with all its buried luxury, all of that was unimpressive from the air. People thought they were going to see impressive buildings, maybe some gold, even though they had been told the whole point was to be secret, hidden. What they saw was a few holes like beetle burrows in the sand, the occasional door-frame waking from a sandy sleep. Everything was below ground, although paths and a visitor's complex had been built for the tourists. Hani's route lay further over to the west, behind the red hills, beyond and behind, even beyond the Valley of the Queens and the workers village, Deir el-Medina. Deeper into the desert, far away from all that. Tradition and tourists, family and future. Enough. God is great. God the Sustainer. Lord of all Worlds.

Baby Cheeks was beginning to sink although it wasn't time for them to come down. They needed more height to get above the turbulence caused by the red cliffs, so Hani opened the burner valves again. Shimmering waves of hot air entered the envelope and Baby Cheeks responded, lifting with a delayed lurch, then continuing to rise. They rose to the allowed maximum – four thousand feet, where the air was colder and he could see his breath puffing out in front of him. He undid his tie and threw it over the side of the basket. The tie curved and rippled like a flying snake, until a sudden draft snatched it away. He unbuttoned his shirt, his fingers cold; it was one of his work shirts and he touched the black and gold chevrons. He had taken exams. He understood the wind and the weather. Ayesha's brothers liked to joke that she thought she was marrying a pilot but she found out she'd got a piece of fruit in a basket.

His chest and arms were covered in goose bumps from the cold. He blew on his fingers until he could undo his belt buckle. His trousers snagged on his shoes and wouldn't pull over them so he sat in the bottom of the basket next to the overnight bag and took off his shoes and socks, one by one. Then he stood and took off everything else. His nose dripped cold water droplets onto his hands and his testicles rose to re-enter his body. Nearly time. He scooped up the pile of clothes and threw it out of the gondola, watching the crumpled pieces separate and drop away from him. His shirt fluttered all the way down to the road as if it still contained arms that could wave, like a fool swimming in the Nile. The last he saw of it, the white material had wrapped itself round the crown of a palm tree and taken on that shape instead of his.

Nobody was going to have anything good to say about this. Except perhaps Ayesha. He hoped so anyway. He was giving her a future, one with children. She would realise that, wouldn't she, once the palaver had died down? Her mother would – Hani knew she had chosen him to spite a friend of hers, one Halima Khan, tall and slim, whose husband had a new Mercedes and whose son had boasted that he would be given Ayesha. They would all talk briefly about Hani's 'accident at work' and then move on with their lives. There was no stopping that family. They were like a sandstorm, an elemental front, charging at life head on. They had no qualms about letting Hani know he had disappointed them. They knew the problem was Hani. No sugar in his cane? No cane? He couldn't face the brothers any more. They were all prodigious breeders with huge numbers of cousins and siblings. Birthday parties every week. It *was* his fault; he was exhausted just by the thought of them all. His mother-in-law was the worst. That woman was everywhere at once, but especially inside Ayesha's mind. He sometimes thought he could hear her opinions about everything from aubergines to politics coming out of her daughter's mouth; she ruled her children like a fat spider on a web.

The voice of a distant muezzin rose up to Hani as Baby Cheeks drifted peacefully on course. It took him a few seconds to locate the minaret, below to the east. It was nearly sunrise. *There is no deity but God,* called the voice. Still looking down, Hani could make out a boy on a white donkey swishing a stick, heading in the direction of some fields. The words of the adhān calling to prayer had no visible effect on the boy. The donkey plodded on, twitching its ears. A skinny boy in a loose tunic, annoying his donkey and thinking about nothing. Impervious. Boys like him were a permanent feature of the Nile. In another five thousand years there would be one just like him coming along in a calico shirt, with nothing on his mind. *Allah is greatest. There is none worthy of worship except All-ah;* the thin voice quavered and ceased.

The dawn was taking on strength now. They climbed to the forbidden height of nearly five thousand feet, as Baby Cheeks crossed the Valley of the Kings. It was deserted down there but would soon be overrun by coaches of sweating tourists, with their sunglasses and their jewellery glinting the sun. At first Hani's eyes had streamed water, but now his eyeballs were cold and dry. He should have brought goggles. He turned his face out of the wind and looked back towards the river behind him. Other balloons were getting into the air, silently rising through the palm trees like bubbles of chewing gum or so many cosmopolitan babies, their multi-coloured heads breaching the mist and drifting towards him.

Hani opened the burner valves to keep Baby Cheeks up in the air current they had found; the burners were fierce, hot on his face and bare shoulders. A glance at the ground told him that they were moving west at a good speed – nobody could interfere now. It was so cold, his body hair stood on end. He shoved his hands into his armpits but they were cold too. He would have to descend a little, or he wasn't going to be able to control the balloon. He fumbled with numb fingers at the flap of a storage pocket, looking for the shaving foam he kept there. His teeth chattered and clamped together at the same time and his fingers wouldn't work the popper. Finally he got it free, jagging and yanking at it. He leaned over the side of the gondola, grasping the freezing metal canister with both hands and squeezing the button. The sputterings of shaving foam dropped like white turds, appeared to hang as they moved in the same air as Baby Cheeks, and then fell into the layers of air below, where they kept up with the balloon until they dispersed. The air at about three thousand feet was also moving west. They could afford to descend a little now.

He wondered again if Ayesha was okay. His phone wouldn't work out here and anyway, she probably wouldn't pick up. He had been shocked. He hadn't behaved very well; he certainly hadn't been any help. It had seemed best to stay out of the way. Hani had sat at the dining table, staring at their wedding photo on the sideboard, blank. He couldn't get the noises out of his mind, animal noises, bovine bellowing that had come from their bedroom. Her eldest sister and her mother had been there with her, bustling in an out and not looking at him.

Baby Cheeks was over the desert now, on the Libyan side heading west somewhere between the phosphate railroad and highway 238 to Kharga. They passed over several dry Wadis. Hani had taken Ayesha to a Bedouin camp by a Wadi for a day once, as a sort of honeymoon. He had heard about these daytrips where tourists rode out

17

on camel back to a Bedouin tent and the women provided lunch in the shade; you could be alone, drinking sweet coffee until it was time to ride back again in a jeep after looking at the stars.

He didn't think Ayesha was going to get on the camel at first. He had been in two minds whether to tell her what the surprise was, but in the end had decided not to. He thought if he told her, she might tell her mother and everybody would have laughed and Ayesha might not have come. As it turned out, she was nervous, which made her abrupt with the guide; she was rude about the hairy stinking blanket that they threw over the scaffold of the saddle. She did climb onto it in the end, and screeched like a cat when the scabby beast lurched itself upright. Hani had stood with his arms up ready to catch her if she fell, but once she was there, she laughed down at him and told him to hurry up. He couldn't recall what they said but they had talked all day long. In the evening, they held hands and chewed flatbread cooked on a hot stone and watched the space station scud across the sky like a neon spider scuttling out of sight.

Naked as a newborn, Hani looked down at the rocky terrain beneath him. He had about fifteen minutes of propane left, but he didn't intend to use it. Baby Cheeks was sinking down to warmer levels and Hani lacked the will to go back up into the cold. His fingers had thawed and he felt the pleasant movement of air on his chest as Baby Cheeks flew towards the Western Desert. The sun had begun to touch his back. God is great. God is merciful.

He vented the parachute valve to bring Baby Cheeks down. The ground beneath them was uneven, a red landscape of rubble and rocks. The basket would probably tip over when it touched down. There was nobody to hold the tow-line. There was nobody there at all. He tucked the overnight bag under his arm and held onto the rope rings inside the basket to brace himself. At the last minute he would squat below the rim, but for now he watched the rocks come closer and allowed the balloon to drift down at its own pace.

The sun is hot on the back of his head. A small beetle crawls past his face and disappears between two stones, antennae bobbing up and down as it negotiates a patch of blood. Hani puts his hand to his face and realises his glasses are gone and his nose has been bleeding. He remembers crouching low, holding onto a rope ring with one hand and clutching the overnight bag with the other, but they had bounced badly. Baby Cheeks had caught a draft and suddenly surged up before dropping again, causing the basket to drag heavily and bang amongst the rocks.

Hani tries to get up, then looks at his hand. He has left red handprints on the earth. He shuffles into a corner and sits in the shadow of the basket for a while, and becomes aware that his skin hurts; it is pitted and raw in many places. He can't remember why he took all his clothes off earlier. It had felt cleansing, but he had been *so* cold. Perhaps hell is a *cold* place; the skin of the sinner burned black by ice, not fire. That would explain all the black, skinless patches on his body. He had imagined himself walking naked into the Western Desert, pure and clean with his son in his arms, but he could have taken his clothes off here. Then he wouldn't be so scuffed and scraped. Stupid.

He unzips the overnight bag and takes out the small bundle he had so carefully placed in there before he left the house. He lays it on his knees and looks at it for a while, wondering if he has lost his mind. *I might have, I might have,* he says over and again. They will say so.

The little body is stiff now. It had been soft and limp when Hani scooped it into his bag. He wants to see his son's face. He wants to kiss the little head and smell the hair, but he knows he doesn't have the courage to look inside the sheet. He knows he won't be able to unwrap his child and then wrap him up again. He finds he is grateful to his mother-in-law, who bound a clean white sheet tightly round this baby. Their fourth. Hani's only son.

Hani tucks the white bundle into the crook of his arm and uses the basket struts to pull himself upright. He is thirsty. His tongue seems scaly, like one of the skinny lizards he has seen skittering away from the basket. He hasn't brought water. What would have been the point? The pebbles cut into his feet as he picks his way over to Baby Cheeks who is still restless, rolling from side to side like a sick animal. He finds the parachute valve chord and pulls hard, forcing air to rush from the crown with a sigh. The pale cream panels begin to fold in on themselves, to snag on rocks, fluttering as if they might rise again. He clutches his son with one hand and holds the valve open with the other until the last of the breath has left, watching until the balloon envelope is a limp flap of skin taking on the contours of the earth. Clutching his bundle he begins to walk, the sun strong on his back and his shadow leading the way.

Orphaline

I walk and walk and when I can't walk any more, I come to this coffee shop. Where I live the people scream at each other, slam doors, leave their music on when they go out. This morning a woman I haven't seen before slapped her child and told him to fucking behave or else he'd be sorry. I was right behind them on the stairs. I wanted to help the boy, but I just stood on my step looking at my feet. He bit his mother's finger and I was glad. She dragged him back up the stairs, leaving the pushchair at the bottom. They were both screaming at each other by then. I had to lean against the wall to let them pass, which I don't like doing because it's dirty.

The coffee shop gets busy later in the day, but most mornings I can sit and they don't bother me. There's a corner I like which is out of the way. I watch the faces. If there's nobody watching me, I can get my postcards out. I have twenty-two. They are all of people, not buildings or scenery. I also have thirty-seven cut out faces from magazines. I have stuck most of those onto card from cereal packets. I don't usually bring all of them out with me. I choose the right ones for that day and put them in my bag. Then I can look at them when I want.

Costa man is often at my table, and we smile, nod at each other. He works on his computer there most days. At first I didn't like the fact that he always comes to my table, but then I was okay with it. He has a latte and then he works. He has a nice face, a bit puffy, as though he eats too many take-aways. He wears a short leather jacket, which is too big for him. He isn't a biker because he wears those red canvas baseball boots, not done up properly, and no socks. After a while we got in the habit of saying – Hello, how are you, to each other. Sometimes we say – Lovely day again. Or – Rain again, hey.

I was careful about Costa man for a long time. I was worried that he was getting interested. Sometimes I would see him looking and I realised I had been going through the faces in my bag or staring at another customer for too long. I thought he might notice my clothes. I only had one pair of jeans and two jumpers then, and I didn't like any of them; I looked the same every day.

One day he bought some carrot cake and two forks and shared it. I just looked at him and ate. It was delicious. He asked my name, and I told him that I didn't know. He put his head on the side but he didn't say anything. He scratched his neck and looked out of the window. My heart was thumping away and my mouth had started talking before I could do anything about it. I told him how I had been found on a mountain. In Switzerland. How kind everybody had been to me but that my memory hadn't come back. They still don't know who I belong to. I would like to get some work of some sort, but my papers weren't right and I didn't even know how old I was.

'What do you call yourself?' He asked after a while. 'I mean, what do you put in the front of your diary?'

'Orphaline,' I said. 'Orphaline.'

He wasn't there the next day and that was worrying: I thought I had scared off the only person who had tried to have a normal conversation since they brought me back to England. Then I thought he had been sent to check up on me, but I didn't know who by or even why I thought that. I always felt somebody was watching, checking what I did and who I spoke to.

A day or two later he was back. Hello, he said. Alright? I nodded and turned the postcards over. He smiled and when he finished his latte, he talked about a friend of his. He said he knew this person who might be willing to help if I needed to try to straighten out my head. She was a therapist who always took some clients she didn't ask to pay. I said I had seen a psychiatrist a couple of times after I was found.

'She'll be more like a friendly person to talk to than a doctor,' he said and pushed a little white card across the table towards me.

The room I have to live in is dark and smells of tea bags and bleach. It came with dirty windows that don't open, cardboard furniture and a stained bed. I can hear other people's music all the time. There is a long thin mirror on the inside of the cupboard door, with a crack in the corner. In that mirror, Orphaline's face looks like a cricket or some other insect. I put my fingers on her thin lips and dark, unblinking eyes. Is she real?

I did go and see Costa man's friend. I left it a couple of weeks and when he didn't mention her again, I rang her. Dr. Gemma B. with a string of letters, whatever they mean. It was okay.

She was calm. She was tall and sat on the front of her chair, elbows on her knees, hands hanging loosely between them like a man. She blinked at me when it was my turn to tell her something. Talking was difficult at first. She said these things take a long time. I wanted to ask her – what things *are* these things exactly?

I am alone. I felt like a child. I didn't tell her everything, even though she said nobody would ever know what was said in her room. I didn't tell her about my plans. It was only when I left her room that I realised I had any plans to hide.

I stopped going to the coffee shop so much after that. I walked. I walked all through Kilburn, looking at faces reflected in the long windows of Woody Grill, the Luma Italian restaurant, the people coming out of the Gaumont after a film. When I came across the canals, I followed them until they didn't have pathways anymore. I walked miles along those concrete ditches with their thick water, all around the zoo and back again towards Paddington. The waterways were busier than I thought they would be and I preferred them to the roads. You could walk a dog here. People nod at you like you are in the country.

I was avoiding Costa man by walking; walking every day, to get away from the habit of him. I didn't want him to ask me about Dr. Gemma; she was getting on my nerves with her questions. Always more questions. What do I think about this, why do I think that happened? When I got in that room with her I just wanted to run. Sometimes I wanted to hit her with the box of tissues she kept by my chair. I could have stopped going but this is what kept me going back – my memory was still blocked and I didn't have the words to unlock it. Who else was going to help me? I thought I would go mad if my memory didn't come back. I didn't have any money. I thought – why can I speak, if I can't remember anything? How do I know how to clean my teeth, how is it that I can do anything at all?

Dr. Gemma said we needed to take it slowly; we didn't know what I could do and what I knew; that is what we were there for – to remember.

I wanted to see Dr. Wallis. I wanted to go back to the mountains.

The memory of the day they found me is still in my mind. It will never soften. I see black shadows of myself, like Pompeii figures trapped in ice. The bar is on the Swiss mountainside, high above the deep cleft cut by the Upper Rhine. The water is the colour of iced teal, tinted by the blue dust it carries with it.

The atmosphere in the bar is thick with Sunday fug, mulled wine, fondue, rösti, lots of pine and stuffed animal heads with glass eyes. Berndt (only I don't know his name yet), Berndt is shouting:

'Hey! Haaallo! Wir machen Schluss jetzt! Alle müssen runter.' We're closing now. Everybody has to go down.

I put my hands out, palms upwards and shrugged at him. A slim blonde woman comes over and looks me up and down. This is Carolina. 'Schon wieder ne Betrunkene?' shouts Berndt across the bar – yet another drunk? but Carolina says she didn't think so. She speaks to me, her voice is kind, worried.

'Madame, we all go down now. It's the end. The little gondola is going the last time for you soon tonight. Where are your skis?'

I look at my feet. I am wearing blue plastic boots. They have chafed sore patches on my ankle bones. I get up. It seems to be what they are waiting for. Carolina comes to the door with me and I look out. There are ski racks outside near a bar cut out of ice blocks. I walk towards the slope, my feet sink into the snow which makes me lurch forward. There are no skis.

'Lass sie mit der Gondel fahren' Berndt says, drying his hands on a cloth. Let her go in the gondola

'Schlechte Idee.' Bad idea. Carolina disappears inside the bar and returns with a radio in her hand. I hear her talking and a crackled response. She beckons me inside again and sits me in the corner with a raspberry tea between my hands, warming them. I don't have any gloves.

Soon a man in a black ski patrol suit with an orange cross on the sleeve opens the door and lets the cold in. Berndt nods in my direction. The man looks at me for a while and then comes over to my table. I get to my feet, knock over the empty tea glass, push my chair back. He is smiling an unshaven smile and shakes my hand. He said his name is Uli. I don't know my name.

I zip up my jacket and understand that I am to go down the mountain with him. The others will ski down when they shut the bar.

On the rescue sled wrapped in blankets and orange oilskin, I feel as though I'm in a papoose; warm and safe. My arms are held against my side by the blankets, but I think I could move them if I felt like it. I want to help Uli who is holding the sled handles, so I lay still and I watch the sky darkening and the shadowy outline of the trees. I hear birds, but I don't see any. It feels like I spend a long time on that journey down the mountain, relaxed, staring at the sky. I don't remember having any thoughts at all. I am calm. Suspended. Relieved somehow, but I might have thought that later.

When we get to the village lift station, Carolina is already there. She is talking to a policewoman who has cuffs and a pistol holster at her buttocks. I think that my comfortable sled has been a clever form of custody. I find I can't sit up or get out without Uli unzipping the oilskin casing for me. I wriggle but he smiles a little sadly at me, his eyes wrinkling, his lips together. He nods, lights a cigarette and looks away, back up the mountain.

The cold cuts into me when Uli helps me out of the sled casing and I can't stop shaking. I have to go with the policewoman and we sit in her small car for a talk. Carolina reaches in through the window, presses a paper serviette from the bar into my hand. It has her mobile number and her email address written on it on it in a cursive script. She looks worried but stands back from the car, watching, her arms folded across her chest. The policewoman is business-like, not unkind, and obviously keen to pass me on to somebody else. I want to cry and blow my nose but I won't use the serviette. What is your name, she asks. Where are you from, England, yes? What hotel do you stay in? Are you with friends here, or husband? Family? Where do you live?

I don't know any of these things. I want to look at the trees and hear the *ssiss* of the snow under the sled again. I say I don't know. Sorry. I can speak German, which surprises me. I speak it well, but not like it is my language, and not with a Swiss accent. I don't know where I learned it.

They are careful with me, efficient. I am given clean clothes and a physical examination. It is decided that I am probably English, from my accent and my physiognomy, although my body gives no other clues as to what has happened to me. A woman called Jo from the British Consulate in Zürich comes and asks all the questions again. I don't have a criminal record as far as they know, so they have to decide if I am mad enough to qualify for their help.

Later I am told they ran my face through their passport system. The system says I am Marion Fowley and I live in Doncaster. I stare at this British Jo from Zürich, featureless in her navy blue jacket, white shirt and sensible shoes. Am I from Doncaster? I have no memory of that town. Jo looks into my eyes, stands up, runs her palms down her thighs, smoothing the creases from her trousers.

'Marion Fowley lives on a small holding near Doncaster, where she has two dogs, some chickens and a vegetable garden. She is the lollipop lady at the local school and has lived in the same house all her life.'

They don't know who I am, I think. I am certain I'm not a lollipop lady from Doncaster.

I have taken the picture of Grace Kelly with me for two days now, but I think it will be the same as all the rest. She can't help me either. I don't know what it is that draws me to them. I find them on my walks, the faces stare at me and I have to buy that card in case it reminds me of someone I used to know.

All the postcards. I stare at each one for ages. I allow myself to choose them for any reason at all, and cut them out of magazines. I don't have to say why I like them. The doctor's surgery has a lot of magazines. I look into their faces and try to see who I am. Am I like this one? Can I see what she can see?

Some of them are men, and I know I am not like them; but something in them *is* like me, only I can't see what it is.

It took a long time for anybody to decide what to do with me. I couldn't help much. I looked at the ski clothes, which had been checked over and returned to me. I put on the ski helmet and goggles and lay back on the institutional bed trying to remember how I got to that bar on the mountainside. I didn't know what day it was or how long I had been in their facility. The food was fine. I didn't know what else to do.

A psychiatrist called Dr. Wallis came. He asked me all the questions again, but he waited to see what I would do. I knew what *he* was doing. He was letting me talk more than the others. Then he said he had seen something like this before, that he suspected I had been the victim of some kind of attack.

'An attack? There's not a mark on me.' I looked down at my own body.

'Drugs. A cocktail. Party mix. You probably had a reaction to the combination.' I thought he was implying I had done this to myself.

'Do you take a lot of recreational drugs?'

'No idea,' I said. 'Can't they tell?'

'Not really,' he said and pointed to my hands.

'Take a look. Do you see anything?' I didn't know what I was looking for.

'I don't get it.'

Gently he showed me the groove on my ring finger, as though a ring had been worn until recently. He also gave me a hand mirror and showed me that I had pierced ears, but wore no earrings – no jewellery at all.

'Does this help? Can you remember what sort of jewellery you used to wear? Do you see it?'

I looked at my left hand. I felt sick. Yellow-greyness spread through my vision. Dr. Wallis told me not to try to remember. It was enough to put the questions to myself; to let my subconscious do the searching. In time, something might occur to me.

I lay down and he took my pulse a few times. Eventually he left.

Another time, Dr. Wallis asked what I thought about the clothes I was wearing when they found me at the bar. I said I must have been skiing and if they had found any bruises, I would have thought I had banged my head and forgotten everything. But then somebody would have been waiting for me and reported me missing.

'That's right,' he said. 'Look at the clothes.'

We got them out and laid them on the bed. I pulled the blue ski boots from under the bed and showed them to him.

'Have you tried them on since you've been here?'

'Only the ski helmet and goggles,' I said. 'I put them on and try to remember.'

'Yes I know. They told me you don't touch any of the other clothes. Why is that?'

I stared. 'What for?'

'Try the boots on. Just, let's see.'

I pushed my right foot into the boot and it slipped in very easily. With both boots on I looked up at Dr. Wallis who gestured that I should walk around the room. My feet slopped and knocked around in them like I was wearing buckets on my feet and I knew they were too big to ski in. These couldn't be my boots.

Dr. Wallis nodded in the direction of the ski trousers and jacket. They were navy blue and matched the boots. They looked big, lying there on the bed – as if a larger person had sloughed off a padded skin, leaving an impression of their body behind.

'We think the helmet and goggles are yours.'

The realisation was a shock in my chest, like someone had stamped on my lungs. Somebody had drugged me, taken my jewellery and clothes and left me on the mountain without any form of identification. The only piece of paper I owned was the serviette from Carolina's bar.

I was lost. Not quite exposed on the mountainside to die, but alone all the same. I wept. I thought my tears would be brackish brown, but they weren't. I thought – perhaps I am dangerous. Perhaps I know dangerous people. Does anybody know me? Does anybody love me? Do I love anybody?

They showed me the wrinkled passport. It had been wet. It had turned up eventually in the resort somewhere and had been handed in. I was told this meant I would be able to go back to the UK. 'This is great news, yes?' I looked at the damaged picture of my own face. The name in it was Marion Fowley. I knew that was not my name.

Costa man was interested in police procedure in Switzerland. He asked me about the policewoman's gun – could she sit down in the car with it on and still reach it? He looked up a list of questions he had thought of and saved on his computer. He was always writing stuff, sometimes about people in the café, sometimes he said it was about me, which made me nervous. He said it was for a film script he was writing but I wasn't really in it. The main character was a man. He had to know everything – if the gun's on the right and she's driving a stick shift, how's she going to draw the gun whilst she's driving? Endless questions like that. Men get obsessed with details; maybe it's the guns they like.

'I'll ask her, if I ever see her again!' I said. I sat back in my chair with my arms folded across my chest. He said, well maybe she was left-handed but they can't all be in Switzerland, can they? Right hand drive's good for something then. I thought it would be good if he shut up. This irritation was a new thing.

He asked me how long I was in limbo there – not allowed to stay and nowhere to go.

'I don't know.' I shrugged, not looking at him.

He asked to see the passport. My hand was shaking as I passed it over.

'It's a bit convenient, isn't it? This, turning up like that?' He looked at it carefully. I stood up hovering across the coffee table, feeling I could snatch it out of his hands if I wanted to. I *needed* that passport.

Faces. The men's faces. Lovers? Sons? Who are they? One girl. Who is the she? Did these empty breasts once nurture one of them? Did they take my child from me on the mountain? Much worse – did I give my child away? Have I done something awful? I dream them, I see them in my mind, reflected in shop windows, go past me on the bus.

I tell Dr Gemma about the faces. They come very often now. She thinks I have made them up from the postcards but I haven't. There are several men but still only one girl. One of the men is lovely. He has ice-blue eyes, which look calm, unshakable – looking at me under strong brows. He has good cheekbones, a week's growth of short beard, very neat, and loose curly hair. I feel that I love him, or would; or did. He looks relaxed, not smiling or frowning. His eyes pull me in. I think he may be my son. Or he may be my husband; or a lover, at an earlier stage in his life. Is this the man I fell in love with in the past? He is too young to be mine now by at least fifteen years.

The girl is pretty, with long dark hair and a red velvet dress. I dream about her often. She makes me feel light blue, like petals of spring flowers or the wings of a bird. She is about fifteen or sixteen and wearing too much makeup for her age. Her mouth is slightly open and her head is tipped on one side. She doesn't look at me, but past me. I like her, but she is busy.

I think she is my daughter.

Dr. Gemma says that because of my dreams, the girl is me. I am not so much looking for my child or children, but for myself – and these faces are manifestations of myself.

I hate her sessions. I probably hate her.

I think the girl in the velvet dress really is my daughter.

An envelope came through the post. I didn't get much post – I didn't know anybody. It was on the floor, kicked behind the door when I came in. I took it to my bed, slit the envelope with a knife. I couldn't speak. My hands were shaking and I balled my coat sleeves up into my fists. An envelope full of twenty pound notes. Loads of them, crinkled, dirty, smelling of sweat and tin. I didn't want the money to touch me, and I couldn't stop crying. What did it mean?

I looked in the mirror on the cupboard door, knelt in front of it, held it steady with my leg. I looked into the dark centre of my pupils, one at a time, and then again, left eye then right eye, but I could only see the light bulb overhead reflecting back. There was nothing else to see. My eyes were empty. I held the plastic bag in both hands, a clear colourless bag, pure and empty. I put it over my head. I watched myself tighten the neck of the bag around my neck, watched the condensation form, the bag fill with moisture until I couldn't see my eyes any more.

At the last moment I peeled the plastic from the roof of my mouth taking what looked like skin with it, releasing the vacuum, not panicking, not caring if I had left it too late. I was grey.

The money comes all the time now. Wads of it arrive in the post. I don't know what I'm supposed to do with it all. It smells of old men.

I think I should know where it comes from and why. I need to work it out, to remember but I can only guess. Maybe it's guilt money from whoever did this to me; my attacker. I feel purple about that.

Then sometimes I think it is my daughter in her velvet dress, trying to keep me safe. She has her reasons for staying anonymous or she would come for me. She needs to do that to protect someone, either me or her. I don't even know how old she is.

Sometimes I think it is payment from the criminals I sold her to and I hold my body and rock backwards and forwards. What would have made me do that? Have I sold my child? I don't even know why I think that.

It can't be right because if I had done that, or had dealings with criminals I might be dead now, and almost certainly they wouldn't pay me when they don't have to. I couldn't identify them – I can't identify myself.

That makes me feel better for a while. Maybe I haven't sold my daughter or done anything terrible. This might all just be a mistake. The money's meant for someone else and maybe they'll come for it one day. When I think of that, my heart stops, then kicks hard against my ribs and I can't breathe.

I lie on the bed and remember the mountains to be calm and to breathe again. I think about the snow in thick beautiful crusts covering everything, making it clean. You don't know what is there, under snow – it makes everything look the same. If there is litter or dog dirt or the most perfect meadow, it all gets evened out by the snow.

The problem is, there are always underground springs that don't freeze, their silver rivulets come to life under the snow, unseen. They start to move down the mountain before you can see anything from the surface, which just looks like normal snow at first. They wash all the dirt away, running like baby eels, down the mountainside until they burst out in rivers, freed from their ice blanket.

I feel guilt when the money comes, but I don't know why. I haven't remembered anything, but I think I *must* have done something wrong if I'm being paid. Nothing else makes sense.

I have realised something: somebody knows about me and isn't telling anybody. Isn't even telling me. My chest is slow and heavy, my throat tight and dry when I realise this. I wonder if it's asthma. I don't go out for days.

I want to walk along the green canals with a dog running ahead, wagging its tail, nosing about in the leaves and looking back to check on me. I want to walk up through the streets of Kilburn, getting bumped into and stared at by strangers. I'd know by their faces that they had seen me.

But I stay in my room. I look at the faces on my cards. I think about the snow, the ice, the pale blue melt-water. The tiny dribbles that wrest themselves free, one by one. They move slowly at first. There is a slight shift where the snow doesn't stick to the earth. It causes layers in the snow. Crystals collapse. It slides a little, becomes more liquid, starts to move and soon the tiny newborn rivulets wriggle under the smooth white crust, looking for a way out, instinctively following their path down to the sea.

I will go out again, soon.

I don't know what to do with the money. I don't have many places to hide all these wads of notes and envelopes. I have put some in the two drawers at the bottom of the wardrobe but I don't have enough clothes to hide them. Some are laid flat under the carpet in the corner by the window where it lifts up but the crumbling underlay makes a blue dust which sticks to everything. The top rim of the wardrobe is deep enough to hide wads of five hundred pounds. I don't want to count it any more. If I put it in the bank account social services opened for me, there'll be questions.

I haven't told Dr. Gemma about the money. I can't make myself tell her, the words don't come out. I did tell Costa man though, one day when he bought brownies for us but I didn't want to tell him how much or what I do with it. I don't think he believed me. He thinks I'm fantasising about being rich although he made some notes in the computer and asked me who I thought it came from. I told him I don't know.

I need to be careful now. I know this but sometimes I want to open my window and chuck all the money out into the road, litter the place with cash like ticker tape and watch the people run around trying to catch the drifting notes, falling like rectangular snowflakes.

I went out today. I went to the electrical shops in Tottenham Court Road, walking all the way up Oxford Street first, a place teeming with life but where nobody lives. I had decided I wanted a computer, like Costa man's. The young Asian and Chinese boys who work in those shops thought it was amusing. I didn't know any of the makes they had and I told them I wanted it to surf the net, which made them laugh out loud. Mostly they were helpful, but I could see they didn't think I was actually going to buy one. They were right. Not there. Also, I would have to get a computer back to my room without the other people in the house knowing, or they would steal it. I would find a broken door, or be threatened with a knife. Or it would just be gone. I gave this some thought and bought a plastic tartan shopping bag from a shop that sold all sorts of bowls and plastic flowers in vases for £1. Then I bought a laptop exactly the same as Costa Man's from a place behind the Kilburn High Road where I guessed they wouldn't mind the cash.

I use it to look at faces. I do an image search of people doing ordinary things like washing up in a proper kitchen or walking the dog. I don't think I had a dog. I am going to ask if I'm allowed one in this house with me, because I would like one. I will look at more pictures to find out what kind.

It turns out I am quite good with the computer, if I don't think about it. Maybe I will remember an old email address and password and suddenly I'll see my previous life; my friend's will pop up and be real. If I knew my real name, I could check myself out on Facebook or Twitter.

I have emailed with Carolina in Switzerland a few times. She is very kind. She said she had been worried about what happened after they sent me home. Apart from the postcards, the laptop and the tartan bag, the serviette with her contact details is my only possession.

Carolina emailed me again today. She said the snow is expected next week.

Snow. Water has so many forms. I can feel it, as though under my skin. The mountains are riddled with escape routes down to the Rhine; the melting rivulets find them all. It is a force of nature, every year; a watery migration. The individual slivers of water scramble through the earth, find each other, join, become small streams, get separated by stones and rocks; always gathering momentum, the water looks for ways to come back together again, always pushing down the mountain side, unseen under the snow.

Today something horrible happened. I was going to Dr. Gemma's, standing in the hall, doing my coat up. I was thinking how to tell her I don't want any more sessions. A shadow like a bear loomed against the door window, the letter box clanked, and with a grunt and some shoving another money envelope dropped onto the floor right by my feet. I nearly fell forward against the door, the feeling I get of grey sweat, the dizziness and yellow nausea rising up my throat and covering my face tight like a wet towel. The person who delivered it had been a few feet from me. I heard him cough.

It was a big envelope this time, heavy, lumpy. A life-sized postcard of Princess Diana was attached to it with elastic bands. It was one of those tourist cards, cut out to the shape of her face like a mask. Curly blonde hair and a tiara. I looked at her face lying on the floor by my feet. She had an elastic band through each earlobe so you could put her face over your face. Her sapphire eyes looked at me. The queen of hearts.

A door slammed and a Portuguese couple from upstairs clumped down towards me, arguing. She gave him a pointed shove in the back and he turned and to show her the flat of his hand, muttering. I bent, grabbed the package and opened the door just in time to let them out, now shouting at each other. They didn't notice me at all.

I walked up to my room step by step and when I got there, I threw the package on the bed where it lay there staring at me. I opened the cupboard, undressed completely and positioned the mirror. Looking in the mirror, never directly at my leg, I lit the matches I keep for emergencies. I pushed each hot stub into my thigh, one after the other in the same place until they had made a blister. Then I lit more and forced the black ends under the skin letting out the water. I made a hole with them till I knew it would scar.

Then I didn't have to think about the money any more that day.

I looked.

I peeled the card off the envelope, undoing its elastic bands, trying not to stare at Princess Diana's eyes. There was a lot of money this time. Big denominations.

Certificates for other money. All spread out on the brown candlewick bedspread. I thought – I will have to do something for this money. Money isn't free.

My legs felt weak, shaky, but I didn't feel pale yellow sick. It was the red that flushed through me. My hands balled into fists, vibrated at my sides and I know that I shouted out. I don't know what I said. I punched the pile of notes with my fists. The bed jumped and the sheets of paper slid to the floor. The horrible postcard fell with it all, the money fanning out in a slow cascade, Princess Diana's face dropped to the floor where the patchy swirls on the carpet would suffocate her.

Then I saw the single word written on the back of her head: 'GO!'

I was quick. I knew what to do. I must have been planning it for days. I bought a sensible bag for the money, and a case for my laptop. I put that woman's passport in my handbag with all the pictures of faces I had collected. I spent the night going over my journey. It was so simple.

Before I could hear any movement in the rest of the house, I opened the door to my bedsit for the last time, peered out and hurried down the stairs. I almost ran to the Quex Road and when the 328 didn't come immediately, I thought I would start shouting. It did come though, and a few minutes later I was on the train at West Hampstead heading towards St. Pancras. I sat by a window on the Eurostar hoping nobody would sit next to me, my knees jittering so much that I had to hold my laptop case on them and push down.

I was in Paris before I felt able to breathe again. Two stops to the Gare de Lyon, with its indoor palm trees and announcements bulleting out of the tannoy. Onto the next train – the TGV – Lyria to Zürich. It was real. I began to think I could control my life after all.

From Zürich Hauptbahnhof, the Swiss Intercity to Chur is simplicity itself. It was dark but I could see the silver and gold lights reflecting on the lake as we kissed its lovely shores and headed up into the mountains. It was only when I got off the bus in the resort, that I realised I had been heading back here all along. Back to the open sky and the clean air, the quiet hiss of tyres in the snow.

It was getting late. My legs felt wobbly and stiff at the same time, like I'd been running forever. I stayed in the first hotel I came to from the coach stop and in that tiny, expensive bedroom, I opened my laptop and read again what I already knew. These were bonds in my bag, they would make me independent. My child had set me free. Who else could it have been? Only the girl in my mind.

I look at my face in the mirror above Berndt's bar and I think – Orphaline looks happy. She is okay here, high up in the crystal air. I watch the families skiing in the last of the slushy snow, and the couples having lunch in the bar, and I think – that used to be me. I think – where are my people now? Do they still come here, ski to the restaurant and watch me without me knowing? Do they recognise me and know I'm okay? My child could find me now. If I stay here, she will know where to look.

At first I expect somebody to remember me. Then I realise that anybody who saw what happened has forgotten it long since. I will only know I have been recognised if I am attacked again. That thought frightens me, especially because I don't know what they did to me. Carolina says they would have already come back, done something, whatever that may be, if they wanted to. With any luck, the time for that has all passed. Costa man's film script will be boring if I'm still in it now.

My room at Carolina's is nice. I like it. Smokey pine. No clutter. It's not too big and I can hear the family moving around me. Carolina's two children are very sweet in a gap-tooth way, full of sibling rivalry and too much television. I will be their slightly crinkly English au pair, when I am not helping at the bar. I only speak English to them, and they go quiet and don't reply. I'll get strict at some point, like an English governess, and they won't be allowed their tea unless they ask me for it in proper English. Or I'll give in and tickle them until they do. I haven't decided yet.

I think about my own child, the girl I see with her beautiful hair and red velvet dress. Is she really my daughter? Who else would send me the money? Who is protecting me and why would they do it anonymously? These are questions I still can't answer.

When everybody's asleep, I look out over the village, up to the slopes shining in the moonlight with the last of the Easter snow and I feel the melt-water running underneath my feet, under the buildings, through the drains and under the roads. I feel it getting stronger and faster, joining, coming together and flowing downwards, on its way to the Rhine, and eventually, after a long long journey, out into the deep North Sea.

Uli came into the bar today. I recognised his black ski patrol uniform first. I was clearing the tables and wiping them with a cloth. I didn't say anything. He might not have remembered me. He got a coffee and watched me for a long time, sipping at the edge of the cup. After a while he came over and shook my hand.

'Hello Orphaline.'

He was very pleased to see me back. He was glad I was at Carolina's. He would be happy to show me around the slopes on his day off, if I wanted, if I felt like getting to know the mountain. Am I skiing again yet? The snow is leaving, but we could hike if I preferred.

I looked into his face. I could see something, some meaning in his eyes. They are pale blue, like the air here; he is radiant brown from the sunlight, like polished cherry wood. When he smiles there are deep creases round his eyes, which leave white lines when he relaxes his face.

I heard a chink of glass, became aware of Berndt drying up behind the bar and trying to fade into the pine cladding. It occurred to me that perhaps I was being asked on a kind of date. I looked at Uli again. He was attempting to gauge my reaction, his eyes moved between my face and the window. Strong hands jammed into his jacket pocket. Good with the mountain, I thought, but not so confident with women. Maybe I *can* do this. I should say something. Just say something. I smiled at him. Uli let out a long breath.

If I ever was any good with men, with people, it's not flooding back. I'm just going to have to take it slowly. Person by person. Take the new chances I am being given. I want to repay the kindnesses that balance out the other things that have happened, the things I know about as well as the things I can't remember. When you have no memory, you have to make your life up as you go along. Maybe that's what everybody does.

Uli and I have been to see the place where the water comes together, emerges as one fast stream, blows out of the granite cliff face and free falls in glorious abandon as white liquid hair, full of air and light. It falls silently, almost imperceptibly and in a cloud of a thousand droplets, hits the living water of the Upper Rhine with no force at all.

Inundation

The Queen Dreams I

They are coming. One by one. Invertebrates! Carrion fish. I feel them. I hear them. They will suck the flesh from our bones.

Anxiety. It worked away at her and as she weakened, it grew stronger. Became panic. Fear. It stuck to her like an anemone on a hermit crab. Had it fused with her skin? She tried to see it in the mirror, twisting her spine this way and that, but it was always just out of sight. She swam from side to side in her chamber, searching, opening doors, emptying drawers, always searching. Everything that she had accomplished might so easily be lost. It was unbearable. She scratched sores that flowered at her touch.

The Queen threw back the doors to her apartment. Pumping her tail, she dredged through the corridors of the palace. Face after face, portraits of the nation's queens. Feud, the fight between contestants for the crown – her crown. That was their way, it always had been. It worked. It ensured a strong ruler but the outcome was uncertain, unpredictable, and above all the Queen craved stability. Stability for her people. If she could only give them that.

The time was close. She felt them in the waters of the Thames. They were coming. They all wanted her kingdom. But most of all, a new four-headed enemy was coming. Their song was on the tide, already triumphant. *Heilallaheilalaho!* The Queen heard it constantly, she would go mad with the noise. Their ululation was always in her head. She – that murdering witch of the rock – with her winning voice and her new alliance of madwomen. Not women, but Nixen – Teutonic water nymphs. Maddest of all.

The Queen swam to a high window and looked down on her terraces. Tonsured hedges of hornwort, ornamental sea lettuces, the Nori gardens and the gently billowing mermaid's fan, all of it began to unravel, the plants detached themselves from their rocks, left the river bed and floated up, up into the muddy waters beyond the palace garden. The ancient perimeter walls crumbled, undermined by a thousand burrowing mitten crabs, who took no notice of her. She looked up to the surface of the water and saw the pits of rain picking away at her boundary, trying to get in.

The old Queen let out a drifting sigh. Her hair floated upright from the top of her head, fanning out like a white seashell corona. Lady Slumpfish patted her shoulder, glancing at the door. They had probably heard again. Everybody was nervous. Stability and succession. The Queen's dreams were a constant source of gossip to the court and to the river at large. Everybody knew Feud was coming. The Minister made speeches saying everything was under control, the Feud would take place in a controlled environment, there were good contestants. All would be well. The press whipped up rumours of rapacious harridans, foreign sea witches and other relatives of the Queen. They speculated on which ones might contest at the Feud and ran profiles of the worst of them, predicting how life would be under their rule. The Minnows took fright, made secret holes in the riverbed and hid their little bits of treasure. If only the Queen would speak to them. But she would not. She would not lie to her people. Trouble was coming and she had no solution. The Queen remained silent.

Lady Slumpfish called her husband. She had asked him to stand on duty in the corridor outside the Queen's chambers and there had been some harrumphing and clinking of spurs, but he had taken the staff of attendance from the duty Captain and stationed himself outside the Queen's apartment without much more fuss. He had pulled a court circular out of his pocket and pretended to read it; when the corridor was clear, he looked over the top of his pince-nez. The Queen's tower was tall enough to provide a clear view down the Avenue Longue, the main approach to the Royal Palace at Battersea. All the guests and contenders would arrive by this path. Slumpfish squinted. He could just make out his Fighting Perch taking strategic cover amongst the tubs of spirogyra that lined the Avenue. He had positioned a squadron of Bass beyond the Great Barrier at Woolwich and out to the Estuary. They would send word of any approach by sea. He put his helmet on a chair and pretended to read again.Lady Slumpfish poked her head out from the double doors to the Queen's chambers.

'Are any of them here yet, Slumpy? News must have got downstream.'

'Not yet, but it won't be long. How is she?'

'The same.'

Slumpfish clicked his tongue and nodded at the Avenue Longue. His wife shrugged and went back to the Queen. A little later, a rowdy school of mixed fry came bowling along the corridor, passing and catching a glass pebble between them. They came to a smart halt in front of Slumpfish.

'Can we go in?'

'When will she get up?'

'I want to see Mamma.'

'Why can't we see her?'

'I have important things to ask her, you know,' said the eldest, pulling down on his waistcoat and stretching himself tall.

Slumpfish hunkered onto his tail fin and fanned them gently. 'Now, now, settle down. The Queen has many things to attend to and when she feels better, she will be very busy.' He dug around in his pockets until he found a bag of wriggling worms, which they eagerly swallowed.

'I will arrange for you to see her briefly, perhaps later today, and then I believe you are all to be sent upstream where the water is cool and clean and there is none of the bother of the city. Won't that be lovely? Now be off with you, eh.'

Not waiting for an answer, he fanned them on their way and; when he was satisfied, he resumed his post outside the Queen's door. The bother of city life was exactly what was coming. The others were bound to turn up any day now and the Minnows had got scent of the chaos on the tide. It could turn into a feeding frenzy. It had happened before.

Extract from the private journals of Slumpfish, Lady Olivia, House of Lamprey.

The Queen dreams every night. She doesn't rest. She hardly eats.

Ministers come with daily reports of the river; everything they say is worrying. Today it was the rain. The press are giving out that if the rain does not stop, the drains will overflow and we'll have another of the Sewerage Overflow Events that plague us. The river will be poisoned again like last year—anybody who can is making a run for it. The fish ladders at Teddington are heaving with eel and salmon trying to get to fresh water. Minnows are panicking. What's more, there are rogue seals patrolling the Great Barrier, catching the fish trying to get back out to sea and snapping at anybody who is coming up for the Feud.

Oşun has showed herself remarkably early, thank goodness. I suspect she has been in town for some time, although she is anxious to avoid delay. Her festival is soon and she will have to be back in time for that. Perhaps the others are also close by. They may show themselves before long. Let us hope Oşun can help the Queen to get through the Feud.

*

45

The Arugba Oṣun, Yoruba princess, virgin herald to the Goddess Oṣun, made her way with great ceremony through the palace corridors towards the Queen's apartment, for all that she was one girl without retinue. Slumpfish had seen her approach. He had not met this one before but his wife knew the family. Excellent news then. Oṣun had got here first.

The Arugba wore a tight skirt down to her ankles with deep notes of purple and green, reminiscent of sunlight glinting through leaves in Oṣun's sacred grove. From her shoulders hung a beaded tunic, which glistened and rippled as she moved. Her bare feet raised little puffs of silt, a crowd followed close behind. Things became complicated when they had to turn corners. That was when they caught up to her and would catch the back of her heels if she wasn't careful. The virgin herald of the goddess Oṣun carried a heavy burden, a huge and intricately carved calabash gourd, which she balanced on her head. She swayed her hips from side to side as she walked, allowing the pull of the tide to steady her, and set off again. It was the same wherever she went, the crowd always trailed behind her but at least at home she had men with whips to keep the people back. Didn't they know that any stumble, *any* misplaced footing would be a bad omen that would last a whole year? Stupid people! Their old Queen does not have a year. Possibly she would not outlast the festival of Oṣun. Still. The Goddess Oṣun, may the cosmos bless her powers, wants to settle a few things with the Queen before it's too late. The Arugba sucked her teeth. Who knew if these perfidious pale fish would honour any agreement when the new Queen came to power, whoever that may be.

'The trick is to make everything beneficial to both sides, my dear.' She could hear Oṣun's words bubbling in her mind. She tried to concentrate on the large calabash; the liquid inside sloshed around precariously. She forced herself to glide – to be smooth and serene, as befitted a Yoruba princess. Her mother could not have done better. Anyway, they weren't offering anything that would benefit any new Queen – quite the opposite as far as The Arugba could see. Oşun, may the cosmos delight in her gifts, must know what she was up to.

The Arugba Oşun made it to the throne room, which had recently been moved to an antechamber of the Queen's bedroom. An old pout-faced courtier was waiting for her and he barred the way, fins outstretched.

'Halt, who stands without?' he bellowed and banged the staff of attendance on the floor, managing a grin at the same time. A hollow *boom* echoed along the palace corridors. The Arugba Oşun imagined they had time to shuffle the Queen out of bed and onto the throne, before the doors swung open. The old boy winked at her. She looked down in case she laughed, which would unsettle the bulbous gourd on her head. She wondered if he was going to tweak her bottom as she passed him, which under the current circumstances would be a disaster.

A reedy voice came from within the chamber.

'Who seeks audience with the Queen?'

'I, The Arugba Oşun, herald of her Gracious Piety the Goddess Oşun, of Nigeria.'

A booming noise reverberated along the floor and the doors swung open.

'Hello dear, come on in,' said Lady Slumpfish, ushering her through the doorway. 'Put it over there.' She indicated a hollowed out pile of stones. The Arugba dipped her shoulder and lowered the enormous gourd onto the pile in one skilled motion.

'Hello Aunty, you look well,' she said and kissed Lady Slumpfish on the cheek. It wasn't true. Lady Olivia Slumpfish looked thin and exhausted, as if it were she, not the old Queen, who was dying.

'Thank you dear. Where is she then?'

'Lady? She's right here.'

They turned to the throne. The old Queen looked like a small fry sitting in an adult chair. Next to her was the regal figure of Our Lady of the River Oşun, Goddess, bending close and speaking quietly to the Queen. Lady Slumpfish could not tell if her mistress was listening or not. She took The Arugba to one of the side rooms, a galley kitchenette, and made them both a cup of tea.

Lady Slumpfish and The Arugba Oşun leaned against the kitchen units and sipped their drinks, Darjeeling for Lady Slumpfish, an infusion of lime and liquorice for the young girl. They watched the proceedings in the throne room through a hatch. In recent weeks, the number of people who saw the Queen was limited to one or two at a time; her nerves couldn't take the strain of a shoal anymore. That in itself was a worry, but there was nothing Lady Olivia could do.

'How are things, Aunty?' said The Arugba. Lady Olivia looked at her properly for the first time and decided she was the most beautiful of an ancient line of stunning women, some of whom Lady Olivia had been at school with. She wanted to catch up on the news. The Arugba and her cousins had schooled in the Thames as well as in the Hudson and some in the Mackenzie, but they never dropped in to say hello to Lady Slumpfish. Nevertheless, she had kept track of friends and their spawn one way or another. The Arugba was impressed.

In the throne room, things were slow to develop. The Queen was tired. She had difficulty opening her eyes. She hid a trembling fin under the heavy robe they had draped over her. The countenance of Lady Oşun, Gracious Goddess of Healing, could be difficult to read at the best of times. As today, her face was often a rectangular page of white cowrie shells from which a whispering sigh might float, carrying an idea, a concept, a picture that entered the recipient's mind, but no real words. The images had to be interpreted by the recipient before they could proceed.

Lady Oşun projected a continual stream of iconographs depicting health and vitality, energy and strength. Eventually, the old Queen seemed to relax. There was a flicker behind the eyelids. It was time. The Lady Oşun signalled for The Arugba. Where was the girl? With a clatter of crockery the girl shot across the throne room, kneeling and bowing as best she could in her tight skirt as she ran over to fetch the calabash. She hefted it onto her head, and brought it to rest again in front of her goddess. In return, she was given a small cage of twelve Oşun Barbus fish to take to Lady Slumpfish, with a nod of assent from the elderly Queen. The goddess Oşun removed the stopper from the gourd. The healing waters within its rounded belly began to rise, to mix like mist with the water of the Thames, covering the face of the Queen. When her head was entirely shrouded in a mixture of the Oşun River water and the home tidal brackish, Oşun stood and crumbled leaves from her Sacred Grove above the Queen so they showered her head and shoulders, falling into her lap through the misty water, all the time humming and murmuring, now louder, now lower. The old Queen closed her eyes and slept. Oşun crumbled the remaining leaves into the gourd, replaced the stopper and swirled it to mix the brew. With a nod she indicated to the Arugba that she should stow the gourd back in the corner of the throne room on its pile of stones.

Slumpfish propped one of the heavy doors open with a stone and leant his body against the other. Even at his great age, he believed it was not done to lean against the furniture in public, but rightly, he suspected nobody would notice. He was exhausted. The party had been going on for three days and nights. If this didn't kill the Queen, nothing would, despite her recent rally. The old girl really had an amazing constitution, coming about like that. On the other hand, Slumpfish could feel his own heart leaping in his chest. All these women in the palace. It was enough to finish him off. He had just closed his eyes behind his newspaper when another troupe of youngsters, hardly wearing what you'd call clothes, sashayed along the corridor into the already crowded throne room. These ones had jewels in their belly buttons. *Maybe I could get a slug from that calabash for myself*, thought Slumpfish as he squeezed himself against the corridor wall to let them pass. A handsome turbot brought up the rear. He was wearing a turban and balanced a large book on the base of his tail. Fanning her face, Olivia came out to join him in the corridor. She leaned against him and took off her glasses, catching her breath. She checked the corridor to make sure nobody was looking. The paparazzi were everywhere these days, always trying to catch one off guard in a less than elegant pose.

'I think this would be the one, if she'd take us on, 'said Lady Olivia quietly to her husband.

'She won't though, will she?'

'No. That doesn't seem to be what she's got in mind.'

'Could get used to the sitar.'

'It's a veena. Like a sitar, but more celestial.'

'Looks like a sitar to me.'

The Lady of the Lost River had been there for three weeks, and the Slumpfishes had to admit, they hadn't seen the Old Queen looking so cheerful for years. A quavering ethereal voice, punctuated only by the occasional strains of her veena, reached them in the corridor.

'Perhaps she'll stay to help, when the time comes?' said the old soldier.

'Slumpy, don't you think I've asked? She says she's never been away.'

'She's not still cross with the old consort?'

'Maybe. She should be above all that really, being the personification of culture and wisdom, or whatever it is they are, she and that swan. It's a messy bird, you know. '

'It was an easy enough mistake to make – Ganga/ Ganges, I don't suppose he did it on purpose.'

'Course he did, the old arse. Anyway, it's confusing her with the Ganges that absolutely infuriates her. Saraswati is quite a different thing altogether. Completely different river. Dried up, you know.'

'Oh bugger, here they come.' The Slumpfishes straightened up as the troupe of dancers left through the open doors, doing that side to side thing with their necks all in time to a vivacious drumbeat, which had started up again in the throne room.

Extract from the private journals of Slumpfish, Lady Olivia, House of Lamprey.

Saraswati appears to have taken up residence. The Queen is delighted. She is feeling much stronger since the visit by Oşun, but we only have half the potion left. We cannot get through to the next festival; the Queen may have three months at most. Probably less.

Saraswati is most charming. Slumpy is quite smitten of course. She says she has been ever present in the throne room and will always be here for us. I suppose I believe that. She appears to have adopted us, Tamesis knows why, although it might be the swans. They've been her traditional mounts since, well, forever apparently. We do have very fine swans here, especially up river. We *may* be able to convince her to stay. Or at least to keep a fin hold. She says her followers are doing fine, they don't need anything more than to know she is with the Queen and that they have each other's blessings, so for now she is content to preside over readings and cultural happenings of the most refined nature, which the Queen is delighted to host. So long as she can get out to the races once a week. At least the old consort isn't at court anymore. He used to fart at these things just to see what they would do; which was nothing.

51

Saraswati says she will manifest until the Feud. After that, she won't say what her plans are. Perhaps she has none.

Slumpy says he detects strains of opera on the tide. Old fool.

It had better not be who I think it is.

I haven't said anything to the Queen.

Extract from the private journals of Slumpfish, Lady Olivia, House of Lamprey.

Lucky we've got the kitchens for it. More of them arrive every day. Some of them haven't even told us they're coming, but what can you do? The doorfish just let everybody in. They had so many 'Do you know who I am?'s and attempted seductions that they've propped the gates open and gone to tea.

Banqueting Facilities Management (BFM) has done a marvellous job with the cellars. Slumpy lent them the Guard and they've put in red leather benches, long trestle tables with cigarette burns on them and ceiling to floor poles for the energetically inclined. They have found a space for everyone. The rest of us can get on with running things while they're out of the way down below. Having a jolly good time, I hear. I might pop down there later, if Slumpy doesn't insist on coming with me.

They all say they're not going home till after the Feud and still more arrive every day. Every Don, Dôn, Danube, Danu, and Dee is here. Tethys has come. She's taken over a whole section of vaulted cove for herself and the Naiads. At least they had the sense to leave the Potamoi at the door although, I am told they are now running wild among the breeding stock on the tide, but the Mayor will deal with that. A night out with the Potamoi – he couldn't be more thrilled.

It's for the best if the chaps stay right out of the way at the moment. Apart from the Rusalki lounging about down there, wailing and wafting and looking for a man to drown, any old Flumina seems to have turned up. All sorts of tributaries.

It's not all bad. The Okeanides are lovely as always; Brackish Doris, of course. Everyone's here. There's one stunning girl with her hair done up in amazing folds, wearing floaty silk robes, the Luo River, I assume; I haven't met her myself. At least Mat-su isn't coming. There's only so much fabulous BFM can handle.

I just told the kitchens to do their best. They're sending out for takeaways like nobody's business and working their way through the Queen's wine at a frightening rate.

The Queen was indisposed, so I had to take Minister's Messages again today – Killer Shrimp have been sighted up at Reading. The Minister says they're invasive, they're rampaging through the country and they'll take over if we don't take drastic measures to oust them.

The situation in the cellars is getting more rowdy. They sit up all night drinking and arm wrestling, for which it is apparently absolutely necessary to bare one breast. The noise is unbelievable. Slumpy is goggle-eyed with it all. Poor boy. I found out he's got his whole regiment serving at the tables. Couldn't stop them.

I haven't told the Queen.

Sequana came visiting. She wanted to pay her respects to Madame. Very good of her, I'm sure. She hooked up with La Somme (Slumpy thrilled to pay his respects) and they essayed La Manche together I'm told. Sequana sat in the throne room on the blue sofa touching up her make-up and pouting gorgeously for two days. It was Dreamtime for the Queen the whole time she was here. Sequana asked me how long *Madame* might be out like that. I was worried she'd think it was a ruse, like something the old consort might have pulled. I gave her my best Gallic shrug. I told her – *The Queen didn't say.*

In fact, we had a visit from two of those Aussie Yawk Yawk mermaid things and *Madame* had to follow them for a romp in the Dreamtime with the Rainbow Serpent – she who created us all, according to the Yawk Yawks. Are they her daughters? The Rainbow Serpent's I mean.

Anyway, the Queen's *Dreaming*. Rather embarrassing but what can I do?

Danu popped up for a chat while Sequana was here. They go back a long way, apparently, jabbering away in their lingo. I offered them both tea. I had some fancy herbal in, but they declined anyway. Eventually they wafted off together and showed up downstairs. According to Slumpy, they're still there, doing shots and cackling uproariously. I lay on the bed next to *Madame* and had a kip. Saraswati said she won't tell. She's terrific you know, that Saraswati.

Have sent to Lady Oşun for more supplies. Word from the Diplomatic Bag has it that the Arugba's thrown her virginity to the wind now the festival is over. Well, she's not the first to feel the pressure. Nobody has got back to me about more potion yet. I was promised some Batik cushion covers as well.

Even I heard the strains of opera yesterday. *Madame* is in denial, it seems.

None of the guests have declared for the Feud. They are *all* to be witnesses apparently. Nobody wants the job. Bare breasted and drunk, to a deity.

Worried Slumpy close to a nervous breakdown.

The Queen Dreams II

The Yawk Yawks have no hands to hold her with, yet she feels carried.

They sing to her in thrumming chants that rumble through her mind, waxing and waning, now growing, now falling back, an ebb and flow of music that throbs in her mind until all she can hold in her head is the rhythm of their voices. On and on it goes.

She begins to see places. Rivers she knows. Then places that she can't have been to. Inaccessible green Billabongs, shining mountain lakes, wide and empty trails of red sand that fill with rushing water and teem with life. In it all is the curving, sliding shape of the Rainbow Serpent, the creator whose shape embodies living water. The Yawk Yawks nod to the Queen. She realises they are beautiful. She hasn't truly looked at them up till now. Their long bodies are shimmering light, their breasts and faces glow with youthful strength, their tail fins are graceful perfection. The chanting continues but now she hears a voice in the back of her mind:

'Listen to the Rainbow Serpent. She has the answer for you. Listen. Listen. The answer is in the Dreamtime.'

Extract from the private journals of Slumpfish, Lady Olivia, House of Lamprey.

The Queen made me take her to the balcony because she had asked the three Ms to come, the Ministers, the Mayor and the Minnow representatives. I knew she was going to give them The Speech. The one everybody gets when they first come to see the Queen. I know it by heart of course, only the end was different this time.

'When I first took on this river,' she began, waving at the Avenue Longue, 'which I was delighted to do – it was my home after all – when I first took on this river, it was a dead thing. Officially lifeless. Ecologically dead. *Now* what do we have?'

She looked over the top of her glasses at them: 'I'll tell you what we have now, a culture so alive and thriving that we have predators again! That's what we have. Even fishermen, I'm told, although they're not the problem. Porpoises, seals, dolphin coming as far as London Bridge!

And we have so many species of all sorts thriving here that the number of predators becomes more varied every day.

And every day we are threatened by the lightening plague of the Overflow Sewer Event.

It was ever thus.'

I wished Slumpy had been with me, the Ms shuffled and coughed. Some of them even talked through it, until the next bit. I gave them the eye. The queen paused until she had their attention. The talkers knew they'd been spotted.

'A time like this – when things are moving fast, changing beyond recognition, a time like this is the best and the worst of times for an established leader to go. However, Succession is the thing. Stability. Future.

The old Feuding is an out-dated custom, I am told. Perhaps they are right. If this is true, then there are no contenders. Only revellers. They have all come to observe but none of them wants the job. Small wonder, actually.

Now I am tired.

Rest assured that although I will soon be gone, I will always be with you. Enigmatic? That's it. You'll see.

Goodbye. Yes, take a digestive with you if you like. Goodbye.'

I opened the doors. The Ministers, the Mayor and the Minnow representatives shuffled backwards into the corridor.

'What was that about?'

'Madder than a flatworm on a hook.'

'Worse than ever.'

'I missed my three o'clock with the ambassador for that.'
'I had a haircut booked.'

The Queen continued with her tea on the balcony and permitted me to sit. Her mind returned often to the Dreamtime. She had a possible solution, she whispered, but it was unorthodox. The wisdom of the Rainbow Serpent was so simple, if you would allow it to speak to you, if you could see, really see – what to let go of and what to keep close. She drifted off to Dreamtime again, to sort out her plan I supposed. Little did I know.

Discordant strains of veena music reached us from the throne room.

'What is it, Saraswati dear?' I called out. The Queen slept on so I put my tea down and went to investigate.

Saraswati held her veena in two hands, her book of wisdom in the third and flapped her face with her fourth hand. She was sitting on her throne of lotus blossom which went everywhere with her, but she looked far from her usual serene self. Was that a spot of grease on her white sari of perfect purity?

'What's the matter? My poor girl.'

'My sister.'

'Really? Which one?'

'Her.'

'Oh dear.'

'Lakshmi. It's always the same.'

'Aah. Miss Moneybags,' I said. 'When did she get here?'

'She's been here all along. It's just taken her this long to get all her jewels and her hair arranged. She's in the garden. Too good for the cellar with the rest.' Saraswati sniffed and wiped her nose with her free hand. 'Everybody is praying to her. Nobody is thinking about the Feud or the succession or about Purity and Discernment and Learning.'

'No. Well, she is very charming, of course, but then so are you Saraswati. *So* are you. Your whole family – just delightful.'

'They pray to her every day, and soon it will be Diwali and I will have to get out of here. I can't stand all that sweet coconut, you know. I'm so sorry.'

'It's the same everywhere I think, they only want culture if it makes them rich,' I said. 'Very few want to be learned for the sake of knowing. But, there is a reason you have endured beyond the drying of your own precious river, my dear. Nil desperandum.'

We sat together for a while looking at the Queen, who twitched from time to time in her Dreams.

'Why don't you go and visit with the swans at Windsor for a few days?' I said. 'I'll let you know when things calm down.'

I didn't tell her about my suspicions – that a distant cousin of the Queen's was on the tide. Not Saraswati's sort, although Lakshmi might get a run for her money, as it were.

Extract from the private journals of Slumpfish, Lady Olivia, House of Lamprey.

A message came today via brown trout from the North Sea. The four of them are on the move. They'll be here in two days at high tide, punctuality being everything with them. I am convinced the Queen has been expecting this. I am outraged. The four of them. Hideous old succubae. Still, if Lakshmi thought she was going to annexe us unopposed, at least she'll have to put up a fight. Charm offensive, as it were. I'm sending Slumpy upstream with Saraswati. His heart won't be able to take it round here much longer. I do hope the regiment goes on manoeuvres as well. Who knows what they'd be like if that lot get their hooks into them. Poor chaps. The Lorelei and the Rhein maidens. What a line up!

The Queen sat me down on the balcony with her today. She wanted a word about 'my punishment'. I told her, I have served gladly. I have never thought of it like that. She said she knew. She said I've been marvellous. I had to snort back a tear at that. She said that after she first came to the throne and a little bit of life was being bred back into the place, the waters clearing up and so on, it was all quite natural, our youthful spirits and so on. Most unfortunate, she said.

Of course that's not the line she took at the time. She was apoplectic then. Rightly so. I could have been exiled. Thrown out to sea. I could see it from her point of view, naturally. She's had to go her whole reign without the ancestral crown.

I hadn't meant to let go of it. Obviously it was just for larks, but when that great cormorant came, massive brute, got his head through the crown and panicked, I tried to hold on as long as I could but I just couldn't in the end. I flew for several minutes hanging on with my teeth. I was terrified. I couldn't see properly. I was freezing. And dry!

It was by the Isle of Dogs when I let go. The ridiculous bird could hardly clear the water. Why didn't it give up? Anyway, we never did find the crown again. Officially, search parties still exist but they're really a tax dodge I expect, dressed up as a patriotic day out. The blasted thing will have been washed out to sea years and years ago. Why did I ever think it was a good idea to go larking about with the crown jewels?

She was very sweet with me. She said I have paid with my service many times over. That I have been utterly, *utterly* trustworthy. That like her, I am an extension of the kingdom now. And for that reason, I will never be free. She said she was sorry that I have to pay such a high price, and then she cried. It was all very sad.

*

They're here. The Queen said she'd heard the *Heihayllallahei* on the tide for some time, so she's been expecting them. The cacophony is extraordinary. All four of them with their long blonde hair that doesn't quite manage to hide their nakedness; it's either *Weiaweiway* laments and moaning or hilarious *Heilahaylllaa Rheingold Rheingold* all day long and her with the voice to drown a thousand ships warbling through the racket. The Lorelei. She's had it with sinking ships and damning sailors, she says. That's not very profitable any more. Also, the Rhein maidens have spent the Rheingold. They blew it years ago. Pity they didn't buy some decent underwear. Anyway, they're broke and it's been *Weiwallallaway* ever since. Our man in Koblenz says the Lorelei had an easy job persuading them they should go global. We should have recruited them ourselves if that's the case. She told them they can bring the gold they make here back up the Rhein and then it'll be the new Rheingold. *Heilaallheiho* and all that. Flosshilde's going to stay here and manage their affairs when they've got enough to take back. Wellgunde will guard things back home while The Lorelei plans their next heist with Bronnlinde. Koblenz say it will be The Yangtze. Perhaps we should warn Beijing?

The Queen's not worried. She says they're welcome to it. I don't think the Ms will see it like that.

The Queen of Tarts and her little Obstkuchen haven't been up here to see us. Perhaps they're not going to. They stormed the cellar with a *Heeiyaheilalalala* and took the bar by force. The Lorelei tells anyone who will listen that in her opinion, the old ceremony of Feud is the best way to decide the future ruler and that she wants and deserves the Thames as well. The Rhein maidens will look after things back home, while she gets a bit of gold going here for their retirement. Everybody is shocked. Even the Dons have stopped drinking although I heard the Volga is past resuscitating. The Rhein maidens have picked out a site out by Westminster Bridge and will wait for any opponents to show up for one low tide exactly, after which time, she'll be *Kveen* here as well. That's what she says. At least our queen didn't have to do anything unseemly to take over. Everybody wanted her. Everybody that was still alive that is, because like she says, the Thames was technically devoid of life.

Anyway, the Mississippi's taking bets. She's got her book set up in the throne room and runners going up and down to the cellars all day long. It seems the Lorelei is the only one who hasn't heard about Lakshmi, Miss Charm and Wealth personified. Well, they don't shut up long enough to hear anything anybody else says, so I can't say I'm surprised.

The Queen is quite enjoying herself. She's got something up her sleeve, I can tell. She says it's to do with the Dreaming and what the Rainbow Serpent showed her, but she won't tell me any more.

The three Ms are hanging around again, ostensibly with an update on the Killer Shrimp situation. I told them we're too busy for that sort of thing. They said there have been sightings of the Lorelei at Westminster Bridge. There are men in suits, robes and wigs lining the railings and the buses can't get past. The Ms seem to think they should have been given tickets. I told them they can't but they said if Slumpy and the Regiment can go, why can't they? Some of the Ms are women. You'd think they'd have more sense.

I'll have a word with the Queen about it. She may listen. On the other hand, she has spent the whole day conferring with Mississippi and is wearing a green visor.

Now we're in trouble. Slumpy and the Guard are upstream. The PM's flapping around like a goldfish with a burst swim bladder, the Mayor is still touring the lap dancing clubs with the Potamoi and the Minnows have gone upstream to prepare their own domestic defences. It's just The Queen, me and the hoard of drunken harridans in the basement. And there's a storm coming.

We got the message from Teddington Weir this morning. They're at the tidal limit already. If the banks flood, it'll mean death to so many. Thousands will be stranded on the floodplain when the water recedes. Sequana said at least it might not be as bad as one of the famous London SOEs (sewerage overflow events) we get all the time, when everybody downstream from the overflow is in mortal danger. Paris sewers are bloody perfect, I suppose.

Still, this could affect the whole river, from Teddington to the Coast. I have alerted the Barrier. It must be raised. With immediate effect.

I have sent heralds to call everybody and say they should come up above Greenwich, or risk being battered to death by the surge of freezing water, which will come pounding into the Estuary with the storm. We have food enough for everybody. Although we may run out of alcohol.

Some people are not yet here for the Feud, but it's too bad. Apart from Mesulina, the feisty Polish Syrenka, it's just the Daughters of Ægir that haven't got through yet and we won't miss them. They've left it late setting off and they're going to hit a steel wall when they ride in on the water hurtling through the North Sea. Can't be helped.

The heralds have been sent to warn people in the channel to hurry up. They must know the surge is coming. Mesulina, came flying in at the last minute as fast as her tail would flip her and just got over the top of the steel plates as they rose out of the water. She threw her silver sword ahead of her and with a powerful surge of her tail she leapt over the clanking metal sheet. Unfortunately she was seen. The men on the Barrier saw her tail, bare breasts and streaming hair and have now taken to the river, safely behind the barrier, as the wild water levels build up on the other side. They're dredging with nets and hooks, trying to catch themselves a mermaid. The Queen has given Mesulina sanctuary in the tower and I have sent the PM a tightly worded message. Meanwhile, I have asked some seals who owe us a favour to bark about near the barrier and put the men off the scent.

It's been a mad couple of days. The storm seemed to focus everybody's mind on the job in hand. The Queen and the Mississippi stepped it up a notch and then closed the books. *Les jeux sont faits* and all that. The Lorelei let rip on her new rock outside Westminster causing ties to be thrown into the air and men to leap off the bridge into the water. The boats from Greenwich also came thundering upriver on this news but when they got there, she'd been dragged under and the pile of stones dismantled by the Rhein maidens who want to concentrate on the gold and leave the men alive. For now.

Lakshmi's been calmly waiting down by Blackfriars' Bridge for them to come and rout her. She's tremendously popular with the chaps and chapesses in the City. They just worship her morning, noon and night. The Nixen from the Rhein haven't show up there yet and apparently they're not going to. They're doing their gold digging round the sources of power as they see it. Lakshmi's declaring that she's the winner, Queen of the Thames. The Lorelei has declared herself the winner, Kveen of the Thames. They don't seem to be getting in each other's way, not yet anyway. I left them to it.

Slumpy's back and so's Saraswati. She wrote some wise poems while she was away and wanted to read them to the Queen. We went to the Throne Room, but she wasn't there. The throne looks different. It has taken on the shape of a venerable old fish. Mississippi was waiting for us. She said the enormous pile of gold under the throne was for us. The Queen said she thought it would come in handy.

'Where is she?' I asked her.

'Oh, she's around alright,' was all Mississippi would say.

I noticed a bright and clever Batik cushion on the Throne. There was a label attached saying 'for Aunty'. There's a picture of a tall girl with a calabash on her head on one side and flowing SSS shapes on the other. I had to try it out. I hopped onto the throne and sat on my cushion, kicking the gold out of sight under the chair. Saraswati nodded and sat next to me on her lotus flower. She got out her veena and I have to admit, I was so exhausted, I began to drift off.

The Queen Dreams III

Throbbing hum of Aboriginal chanting, like a thousand dragonfly wings hovering above water. I saw the sky and the land and the snaking shape of the rivers of the world as if from above. I flew again, like when the cormorant carried me over the Thames and I was above the river, only this time it was me who was flying. I began at the source and followed its meandering, ever widening silvery path as it gathered villages and towns and locks and palaces to itself. Then came the majestic buildings of men and the shadow of commerce, a knot like a blockage in the bowel which then disgorged into the sea. The silver helmets of the Thames Barrier were like knights guarding my realm; the estuary was a wash of mermaid hair blown in the wind. The sea rippled and shone, and white beaked dolphins leapt to greet me. And I leapt with them and dived into the silky water, and with a ripple of my body, I was speeding back upstream to my castle. I proceeded up the Avenue Longue, passed through the silent portrait corridors and came to rest on my throne. The Old Queen was there. She had white streaks painted on her cheeks and she held a flexible spear in her left fin. She chanted a long song that set my mind thrumming and her dance was a slow rhythmic slide and shuffle that brought her to a standstill behind me. She wrapped her fins round me, gently holding me and I knew then that she had become the throne itself. She was not leaving. She did not die. She had absorbed the power and the mystery of the Dreaming and become part of the past, the present and the future, which are all one thing. She whispered to me:

'I am so sorry, Olivia my dear, to do this. You have earned rest and retirement, but the best of us never get it. You are too good for that. There is nobody else who understands. Except Saraswati, and she will help you. Let them have their aspects of the Thames. The Lorelei can hound the politicians and they will throw scraps of gold her way. Lakshmi can be the darling of the city. You don't want that anyway. You are the centre. The essence of it all. You are the embodiment of Tamesis now. '

She stroked my cheek with a soft fin and in time, solidified into the form of the Trout Throne. The thrumming of the chanting faded. Strange flat zigzag newts scuttled for cover under flat stones. The rain picked a staccato tune on the surface of the water.

And I knew it was true. She had been training me for years, but I hadn't seen it. I sat on my cushion and looked at Saraswati. She didn't seem at all surprised. She tuned her Veena, plucked the stings and tightened the keys until she was satisfied and then she sang her favourite lyric to me. It was about a swan who could tell the difference between milk and water and when given a mixture of the two to drink, was able to sip the milk and leave the water in the saucer.

After a while, Slumpy came in. 'Hello fruit,' he said and kissed me on the cheek. He wandered over to the Throne Room kitchen and after some banging around, he tottered out with two china cups on a delicate tray.

'Tea?' he said.

Cenotes

(/ Si-nō ti/ A deep natural hole in the ground with a pool at the bottom of it, especially in the Yucatán Peninsula, often used by the Mayas as a place of sacrifice
— The Chambers Dictionary)

I

Ramón glanced into the deep shaft, took the towel from his father and stepped backwards into the dark; carefully wiping each rung as he descended because when it got wet the ladder could become dangerous. If the clients fell there would be trouble and his father, Pedro Garcia Hernández, the best dive fixer on the whole Yucatán peninsula, would lose face and maybe money too. They had a big group of Germans this year who were filming their exploration of the region and all the gear had to come down this narrow shaft, everybody balancing on the rickety ladder. It was early morning, just before dawn and Ramón had to be quick because other tourists might also come soon and then Pedro's divers wouldn't have room for their equipment on the platform below and then the beautiful woman diver they had brought with them might complain about him. Serena, like the elf queen, tall and elegant, with her long blonde hair and eyes that missed nothing.

This particular Cenote was different – important. Ramón hadn't been to this one before although Papá knew them all, even the secret ones and the ones on private land and his brother Miguel had been to most of them too, when he helped in the business. It was creepy, this one. It was a large hollow filled with purple light, penetrated by two shafts of mist that reached into the cave through ragged holes in the earth. He knew one opening was directly over the water because he had looked down at the lake from the surface above when they had been getting the

66

dive gear together. The other hole was over Ramon's head as he climbed down the ladder, which ended on a slatted wooden platform laid over some rocks. This is where the divers would get ready before the dive – where they spread out their nitrox tanks, the regulators with metres and metres of black tubing that Ramón had to lay out carefully so they didn't get damaged, the motorised water scooters, the torches and backups for everything and then did a final inspection under the camera lights.

As he climbed down through the limestone shaft, Ramón's eyes came level with the cave roof. He could just make out the small bats huddling together like ripples of moss blanketing the rock face. Descending further a beam of powdery light on the other side of the cave reaching through the damp atmosphere down to the lake. Where it entered the surface, the light became a shaft of pale turquoise piercing the dark water.

Ramón felt he had entered a dream. He lost track of time, climbing down the ladder, looking at the pale beam of light entering the water, wiping each step; when he reached the bottom he hurt his foot on the floor because he wasn't expecting it to be there. He looked about the slatted platform and noticed more steps down to the water on his left. He moved carefully to the water's edge, gripping the slimy surface with his toes. The beam of light was turning from silver to pale gold.

'Fuck, that's beautiful' he said out loud and felt his mother's hand cuffing the back of his head although she would still be making breakfast at home.

Ramón thought he should call up to the others and tell them they could come down the ladder; he thought of all the feet clattering onto the platform, the voices echoing around the cave, the smell of sweat and sun block changing the cathedral atmosphere of this place. He breathed in deeply, lowered himself to sit by the purple lake and allowed his feet to dangle into the water. It was cold and soft; grit and slime fell away from his feet into the water in little clouds of ash.

Ramón's aunt, Magda Estrellita, liked to tell him about the water in the sinkholes.

'The whole of the Yucatán peninsula, our land, has no rivers,' she told him, 'not one. Amazing, eh? Not in Campeche, not in Yucatán and not in Quintana Roo. In this region, the gods made the rocks special, very unusual, they are too porous for holding a river, so the water slips down into the body of the earth.' Magda Estrellita worked as a tourist guide at Tulúm and was the family authority on all things Yucatán, especially everything to do with the old religion.

'The cenotes fill up with groundwater, which comes from the rain.' Here she would do a little pattering motion with her fingers which people found themselves copying. 'They are all temples. Very sacred. The goddess allows the water to collect in these places in her body, which become hollowed out by the water. This takes a long time; meanwhile the goddess sleeps. Sometimes the water withdraws, the roof collapses and her secret purity is exposed. Man finds her, and she allows him to plunder her so he may have water for his own purposes, to swell the grain and feed his children. But nothing is free and they had to make sacrifices. You know what they sacrificed, in those days, hey Ramón? Bad...little...boys.' And then she would knock on his forehead with her knuckles.

'Eh, Strellita! Don't tell the boy this shit,' Papá said, but she just laughed and ruffled Ramón's hair.

'No, really,' he said, 'Rosa will kill me. Or you.'

Ramón's mother was famous for her violent temper, probably in the whole of Yucatán, but Magda Estrellita just laughed again. She and Rosa had locked claws long ago.

Ramón dangled his feet in the lake, his finger running along the edge of the platform. The wood was slimy from sun block, which the tourists were not supposed to wear because of the special ecosystems that every single cenote had, but they did and if it got busy, their perfume made the water taste of chemicals, like the air in Cancún; like money. He thought of the fish, dark and strange, shadows in the deep cold. The dust of human stench must drift down to them and disturb them in their sleep.

A little frog jumped its tiny cold pads onto Ramón's leg, felt the heat of him and leapt sideways into the darkness. Trying to see where it had gone, Ramón stepped onto the ladder that entered the water from the platform. He dropped down to the next step and to the next until his legs were fully in the water, cool and still against his crotch. He looked around the cave to confirm what he already knew. He was alone. His eyes steadied themselves on the beam of golden turquoise light; he slid his body down, pushed off from the steps into the water. It tasted clean, and mildly of sulphur. All the cenotes had their own taste.

Ramón had swum alone before, although it wasn't allowed. His father didn't think it was safe; his mother wouldn't pack his swimmers – it was one of the few things they agreed on. The water was dark, thick; he couldn't see his own feet. He knew none of the fish were dangerous and they slept at the bottom anyway. Little guppies might flit around the edge but nothing would be here that might hurt him. This he knew for sure. There were not even any plants to grasp at him with slimy fingers – it was too dark for plants. He knew this, but as he cast his body into the water, released all connection to the land, a shiver rippled through him. His scalp began to prickle. A familiar premonition came over him, of something big rising up from the depths to take him, to pull him into the dark and slip him between the crevices, pull him behind the rift walls of the cenote, where he would discover its secrets and really be within, like the divers. Ramón kicked his legs causing a mess of turbulence that chased him across the dark, towards the beam of light. Colder water moved across his thighs and belly. He knew the monster fish was rising, blind with questing whiskers, he felt the swell of its body moving towards him, displacing cold water with its bulk. It was happening, the rising-up of the monster the eel, giant flat-headed catfish eel that he dreamt of. He struggled towards the light and had to pull up hard when he made it so he didn't overshoot. Panting and sweating despite the cold, he looked around himself in all directions, twisting himself around and around looking in to the water either side of the precious beam of light. Nothing came.

Still panting, Ramón looked up to the domed ceiling of the cave. Fibrous roots dangled down towards him. He felt as if he was inside a skull and some god had bashed in the bones with a club so that hair poked back through to the interior along the cracks – the wound was right above him, letting in the light. He stayed within the beam of light. Safe. His breathing slowed and he rotated his body in the water, slowly, looking around, searching the dark water.

No monsters would dare to come into the spangled turquoise water. They would stay in the purple-black, for sure. He shivered. The dark water seemed to thicken a little, to push against his pure beam of light. Now he was sure of it – something else was in the water. Not the eel monster. That had probably sunk back down into the deep dark. Long bodies were swirling round him in the water, a disjointed mass just beyond his vision. They didn't come into the light but he knew they were there, he could feel them all around, churning the water. It should have been absolutely calm. They swirled around him in milky clouds. Spirits of the dead? Sacrificed boys of the past? Or spirits of the goddess – manifesting, moving through the water, boiling around him to make him see? Ramón was panting hard again, snatching his breath; he twisted, trying to tread water, to hang vertical with his mouth and nose just above the surface, his eyes slanted towards the depths. The pull around him increased its pressure, the swirl of the water spirits circled faster; they were drawn to the light, its sliver dust and life-giving beauty. They fed on it. They could smell his sweat, taste his life cocooned in the beam and they wanted him. They were separated from him by a membrane, silky thin, pliant as rubber. If they pushed against it they would be able to feel him, grab him, pull him out of the shaft of light. Ramón turned his eyes to the circle of light above him and he saw – blue sky. Day was here. He saw the foliage rustle and dip at the edge of the hole. A face peeked over the top, half obscured by leaves. The person was shouting; Ramón's ears were in the water, he couldn't hear but he knew the face was shouting. Keeping his own face turned up towards the sky, he rotated his body round to the entrance platform. He wanted to look at it to see if the others had come, but his eyes were fixed on the place in the roof where the face appeared. If he looked across, looked down, the spirits would gain in power, strength would be given to them, they would be able to cross the boundary between purple half-light into his pale haven and the goddess would claim him.

Estupido! Ramón. Ramón. Get over here.

Papá! He looked. Papá was setting up the lighting array and Ramon could now hear the old generator that powered it throbbing somewhere on the surface. The Germans shouted up and down the ladder shaft to each other and passed bulky apparatus down to the platform. A cold current brushed his skin again, a cool draft from the depths of the world. He shivered.

'Fuck that,' he said out loud and swam like a demon, panting and plunging his arms into the water, pulling himself nearer the loud, warm people until, through the blaring light he saw his father's hand reaching out to him. Firm fingers clasped his own, then his wrist. Breathless, he felt his father's wiry strength haul him out of the water, his feet slid sideways and despite his father's hold on his wrist he banged into somebody who was carrying a pile of fins.

Serena. She touched her leg as if stung but didn't look at him. Papá held him so close that for a moment, Ramón felt his own fluttering heartbeat damp against his father's chest.

'Ramón – this is work. Don't do this shit, Ramón.' Papá looked into his eyes a little worried but cuffed him over the back of the head all the same.

Shivering, Ramón sat on a rock towards the back of the platform, out of the way, between the sweating limestone walls and the activity on the stage. A man with colourless stubble for hair got in front of the camera, his mask raised on his forehead – it was Horst, the boss. A smaller man stepped forward to adjust the mask, which had been glinting in the light too much for the camera. A discussion ensued about whether Horst should remove the mask altogether, perhaps holding it in his hand so, or possibly so. Horst decided to keep the mask on his head, so in the end they adjusted it and started again. Ramón picked at his shorts, which would stiffen to cardboard as they dried. The stitching was coming apart and Mamá would be mad at him for swimming in his clothes again. Papá would definitely give him a slap with his belt for embarrassing him at work. 'Fuck that,' said Ramón to himself and rested his head against the crumbling cave wall.

II

There was a slight ripple, a change in the water and Ramón knew the divers were returning. White light from the torches appeared in the water at the back of the cave. People said the passages were very long, very deep, filled with water that connects with other caves and some said, deep down at the bottom, the waters connect with the sea. The divers wanted to extend guide wires far to the back of the tunnels and had taken a lot of equipment with them that day, scooters and their rebreathers, which made Ramón feel he would choke just thinking about being down in the dark, reusing your own breath. The weight of the earth, metres and metres of it on top of you, and all that water pressing down on your chest and crushing your skull, pushing in on your temples, and all in the dark. His breath left his body when he thought about it. Ramón saw several torches now, emerging from the folds in the side of the pool. He knew that they always had backup torches, and backups for those, but he swore for the thousandth time that never, never in his life would he go cave diving. The goddess could take them anytime she wanted but it seemed blond foreigners did not interest her; the giants were back safely again.

They had been lucky today, no tourists had come to spoil everything. The divers rose to the surface black and bloated, one under the other. They made almost no bubbles because of the rebreathers; it took them a while to adjust, to normalise their breathing, removing their rigs from swollen bluish lips. They wore full-length wetsuits with thigh pockets bulging with tools, wire, knives, and pliers. They switched the scooters off underwater and handed them up to Papá, who heaved them carefully over to a towel where they rested, like a catch of tuna fish laid out on a boat.

Horst was the first to surface. Ramón was ready; he had brought his sisal basket of towels to the edge of the lake for the divers. This was another part of his job – to keep the fresh towels coming and take the wet ones back to the truck. Papá reached out his hand, braced his feet and leaned backwards, counterbalancing the weight of this huge diver who was suddenly out and upright on the platform. Horst removed his dive hood and scratched his pale stubble, looking at Ramón. Ramón looked away. This man was too huge. Not fat exactly, but enormously tall and heavy; he was always serious, intensely bound up with the dive, but he often looked at Ramón. Ramón didn't like this man – he was too – colourless. He picked at the seam of his shorts and kept his head down. Horst could get his own towel from the bag. Papá was going need help with the equipment soon enough. Everything had to go back up the ladder to the surface to be inspected, recharged and cleaned before tomorrow's dive.

Serena was the last to surface. He knew it was Serena because of her long legs and slow graceful movements, a ballet dancer in a dream. She brought her scooter to the edge and Ramón scrambled to get it as she unclipped the D-ring from her waist and lifted it towards him, helping him to get it out of the water. He laid the torpedo out on the towel at the edge and turned back to her as she reached her lamp and batteries up to him. Then she placed her hands on the platform and with a *hup*, was on her feet beside him. Ramón passed her a large towel and then the smaller hair towel he kept especially for her and went back to his corner. Serena smiled in his direction, stood with her hips thrust sideways as she pulled off her dive hood and scratched her scalp, talking to Horst – about one of the guide wires that was coming loose as far as Ramón could tell. Horst put his hand on her shoulder; he wanted her in front of the camera apparently. She had no problem with that, wore no makeup and her eyes did not waver from the lens. Ramón thought of his lumpy sisters. They couldn't even answer their cell phones without makeup although they only talked to other girls. He was the only one in his family without his own cell phone. Miguel had got his when he was Ramón's age, earlier probably. Everybody had one. Except Maria Fernanda and she was too young. He should have his own cell phone, like his friends, like everyone.

When Horst was satisfied with the film the divers sorted through their gear, yards of black tubing and gunmetal tanks glistening in the stage lights, to the distant throb of the generators. There was no need to rush. Some divers ate a banana or a sandwich; others stacked the tanks near the steps. Serena dropped her wet towels into the bag that Ramón had to drag up to the surface later. She stood near the edge of the platform looking at the water and removed her neoprene suit. Ramón knew she usually wore a sporty swimming costume with straps crossed between her shoulder blades and cut high up her thighs. He thought she might wear a bikini one day. He was not the only one pretending not to notice her delicate hairless skin as she stretched her neck and shoulders.

Serena stood with her toes curled over the edge of the platform and looked across the cave. Her eyes fixed on the central beam of light and the turquoise shaft reaching down to the inky water, her head tilted to the side. Ramón thought she must have seen the beam when she swam back to the cenote through the dark, it would have led her back to where he and Papá waited. She must have swum through the spirits. She probably couldn't feel them with all her equipment, her thick suit and the motor running on her scooter – she wouldn't know what was in the water with her; she didn't know about the goddess and her monster. Don't go in, don't let her go in, Ramón whispered to himself. Don't. They will take you if you allow your skin to touch them.

With a sudden movement she dropped forward from the platform, feet first into the water. The other divers looked up and then went back to what they were doing, a lack of concern that astonished Ramón. He ran to the front of the platform, saw her on her back in the water, long blonde hair radiating around her, looking up at the roof. Her eyes found the hole to the upper world and with slow kicks she moved towards the beam of golden light. Ramón felt his chest tighten. He tried to swallow but couldn't. Don't go over there. You should stay, stay out of the water. You shouldn't be here. Look at you with your hair. You are wrong here. Wrong. Wrong. Even your legs are wrong. Get out, get out. Get out. Ramón began to tremble. Standing on

75

the edge, he thought he might fall in but he couldn't help himself, he couldn't step back to safety.

With a twist his father caught him by the shoulder and turned him away from the floating woman.

'Nice eh, Ramón,' he whispered close to Ramón's ear. 'But not for you. Do the torches. Start getting them up to the truck. Now.'

Furious, Ramón shoved his father in the gut, unbalancing him. He heard the rustle of the bats again and they were saying '*Get her out, get her out, get her out.*' He turned to look at the water as his father caught his arm and saw that Serena was in the beam of light looking into the sky. She was a golden angel, with long limbs and long hair for wings, suspended in unearthly perfection. His father tightened his grip hurting him as Ramón struggled, kicking at his father's legs. He shouted to Serena.

'Get out! Get out now! This is not for you.'

The sweep of Ramón's skinny arm took in the water and the cave but she didn't hear him. Her ears were submerged and she remained motionless, looking at the sky. The other divers stared at him. He was shaking all over.

'Get out! Get out!' shouted Ramón again, not daring to take his eyes off Serena. His father grabbed his shoulder and pulled him away from the water. Horst stared at him, a look of distaste in his grey eyes.

'Ramón, you are sick. You are hot and shaking,' said his father loud enough for the divers to hear. 'Go up and wait in the truck for me. Maybe Miguel will come and get you later.'

Ramón registered the disappointment in his father's voice; he had expected more anger. Chin on his chest he nodded once. Without looking up, he hefted his bag of towels over his shoulder and began to climb; blood throbbed in his ears as he passed hand over hand, on and up out of the dark. He had heard the goddess and she didn't want the foreigners here. They must get out of her temple, out of her body. He must get them out and make sure they never came back. This violation, this *sin*, must not continue. Papá would understand in the end.

Ramón slid into the front seat of the dive truck. Maybe he *was* sick. He might be in another dream. The trees above the truck had been alive with birds when they had parked early that morning but they were silent now that the day was heating up. Ramón pushed his fingers into his armpit and felt its wetness. His neck and face were sweating too. He leant his head back on the seat, closed his eyes and saw Serena splayed out in the water, a sacrifice to the water goddess, to the flat-headed avenger sulking in the depths, and to the spirits circling in the purple water making it thick like milk. And she was helpless, for all her strong limbs and beauty.

'Fuck. Just go, woman,' he said out loud.

Horst's face came to him, luminous white skin, grey eyes looking him over. Ramón sat up straight. They were weird, those German divers. The cenotes are beautiful, jewels of the Yucatán and there were many visitors every year, but these divers were different, going too deep into the goddess' secret places. Maybe there would be trouble for Ramón and his family for helping them. That could happen. The gods of the Yucatán did not show mercy.

He allowed his head to relax against the seat and released his breath; he tried to imagine the dark folds of the caves parting, accepting the divers. Maybe a deep cenote could get angry with the divers, boil and twist up like a tornado, explode with anger like the fury of the devil himself and all these rubber clad foreigners would get spewed up high into the sky, pam, pam, pam, one after the other, thrown up so high they would have a full view of the whole of the state of Quintana Roo, right across the Caribbean sea, suspended high over the whole Yucatán for a weightless moment like the instant at the top of a swing, before wet, black, heavy – they plummeted down, trying to angle themselves for re-entry into the cenote that had expelled them, but the goddess wouldn't want them so they'd just crash to the ground, smashed, heaps of broken tanks, glass masks, contorted limbs.

Ramón jerked awake. His father's hand was on his forehead feeling his temperature, his mouth close to Ramón's ear.

'You make me crazy. Do you want them to call that cheating cabrón Ernesto to run the dive for them? We have to eat – and you,' he sucked his teeth and slapped Ramón's head, 'you will take the food from our mouths with this shit of yours.'

Pedro shut the truck door and stalked off across the car park, his boots crunching on the gravel. Ramón sat in the front of the truck. Occasionally he looked round, but didn't dare get out and help. The truck jolted every time a tank was loaded in the back. Impossible, how all this equipment could drift through the water to the secret places of the earth yet was so difficult to carry the rest of the time. The driver door opened and Pedro got in, shunting forward to reach the pedals. He gave Ramón a look and spat the matchstick he was chewing onto the dirt outside.

'Miguel is coming. He'll get you from the motel and he'll take you to Mamá.'

'Papá – I...'

'No. You will stay with your mother until you can be a man and work with me.'

The truck emerged from the jungle track and turned onto Highway 307, crawling to join the traffic. Pedro looked in his mirror for the air-conditioned Chevrolet Express they had hired for the Europeans, driven by Andrés who was an elderly cousin of Magda Estrellita. The motel they used as a dive base was about forty-five minutes from today's cenote. Ramón liked it although it wasn't fancy; it had whitewashed huts dotted around the restaurant hut, which had a bar at one end. Near the car park was a long rectangular hut with green strip lighting, a TV and a pool table, guarded by a thin youth called Gustavo who constantly rocked his body to music from his earphones and kept a cigarette behind his ear; he was the receptionist and was only polite to the foreigners, and to Magda Estrellita to whom he was extra sugary, a thing Ramón found horrible to watch.

Everybody got busy rinsing the gear with hoses, hanging suits to dry, storing equipment in the locker room whilst Pedro unloaded the heavier pieces onto a wooden trolley, helped by Andrés. All the while Ramón stayed out of the way, his chin on his chest, listening to the activity around him.

The divers wanted to spend the rest of the day mapping their dives. Horst placed a whiteboard on a chair in the lunch hut near to where Ramón was finishing his sandwich at a table in the corner. Pedro nodded him back towards the truck but Ramón dawdled over his food watching the divers push some tables together, which they soon covered in maps, photos of the cenotes and other facts and figures. Some of the divers wanted to take a trip to the other side of the peninsula to take a look at the cenotes near Mérida although filming in the deep long caves of Quintana Roo would remain the focus of their trip. They asked Pedro about access to the remote cenotes, which were deep in the jungle. Some would mean a train of burros and a long hike, but it was no problem, for them he could do it. He knew a man who, with a little notice, would hire up to twelve burros. Other cenotes could be accessed by the old sisal railways that still existed on old plantation land from before the war. Also, Pedro had heard that his sister Magda Estrellita might take them on a night visit to Tulúm if they stayed this side, if they wanted it. It's not allowed of course, but she is a guide, she has connections, which means they would have to pay – but it's no problem, if he called her.

Pedro shrugged, lifted some Coronas out of the cold box. He passed them around while the Germans talked things over; he knew how to fish.

Andrés ambled over to pass Ramón a Coke with fat, womanly hands.

'Hey, you'll go blind. Didn't anybody tell you?' Andrés winked at Ramón who had cupped his hands over his crotch, suppressing a need to pee. Ramón took the Coke with one hand and placed it by his plate.

'Gracias.'

'D' nada.'

Andrés nodded to the carpark – Miguel was sauntering across the gravel, his legs skinny and bandy like a road cop getting off his bike.

'Come on idiot. I have to be back at the hotel later. Let's get going.'

Ramón followed his brother back to the dive truck, where their father was waiting for them.

'Miguel,' he said. They clasped hands and embraced, chests touching for a moment. Pedro cupped his hand behind Miguel's neck. 'Ijo. How is it?'

'No problem, Papá.'

'Bueno. Take this useless one to his mother. I didn't have time to call ahead. You call her,' he said, pointing at Miguel. 'Say I will come tomorrow night after the dive and if he is ready, I will bring him back, if no, she will keep him after all.' Without looking at Ramón, Pedro returned to the divers brushing the boy's head with the palm of his hand.

Miguel grinned, his eyes on Serena as he crossed to his flame-coloured SP2 Classico, shoving Ramón in front of him. Ramón kept his eyes to the ground but ran his finger round the chrome bumper. Miguel clicked his tongue and knocked his hand away, still looking at Serena. When he was in the passenger seat, sitting low so he could hardly see out of the window, Ramón checked the faces in the restaurant. Serena was talking to the cameraman, Lutz or something he was called; she didn't look very interested. Miguel spun the steering wheel with the base of his palm, picking up speed and scattering stones across the parking lot as he turned the car towards the road. At the same moment, Horst stepped out from between two cars. He watched them leave, following them with his empty grey eyes.

'Jesus! What an enormous fucker,' said Miguel. 'Is he part of the dive?'

'He's the boss.'

'Jesus. Like some fucking ghost.'

'I hate him.'

'Oh yeah? Hey, how come you are so fucking useless, Ramón?' Miguel took a left and settled into the drive to Valladolid along the Coba Road.

'Fuck off. *Brother.*'

Miguel cuffed him round the ear and lit a cigarette, his elbow out of the window. 'I am supposed to see friends in my time off you know. Not drive stupid little fuckers to their Mamacita. I work hard.'

'Bullshit.'

'Fuck you. And fuck Valladolid.'

'You want to break your mother's heart?' Ramón mimed two hands crossed over an enormous left breast and a look of sanctified pain, which had Miguel roaring with laughter. 'Oye! Call it Zaci. Did I raise a pig for a son? Home is Zaci my son.'

Miguel turned up his music and they drove without speaking for nearly an hour. He picked at his skin and smoked continuously. Ramón leant his head out of the window letting the wind freeze his forehead. Some of his friends might be around tomorrow; they might all play football after church, if they didn't have to go straight home, which Ramón almost certainly would have to. Maybe he could get away for an hour.

'Hey, Miguel.'

At the same time Miguel said – 'I have an idea.'

'Shut up idiot – listen to me,' Miguel thumped Ramón's thigh with his fist. Ramón sat still. He looked out of the window rubbing his leg while Miguel talked. It was like this. Miguel was doing fine, real good, but - he had some friends who had money. Real money. There was more money in Cancún than a boy from Zaci could imagine. These friends wanted to help Miguel and his family. They sometimes need to hide things, see. Packages. Not to be opened. To be hidden. You don't discuss this with Papá and he won't say anything. And don't tell Mamá.

'Don't tell Mamá what?'

'I told my friends they have to pay you. What about that, Ramón? You will be earning money. Soon. '

'You will, you mean.'

Miguel wagged his index finger at Ramón. 'Our family. See, I will share my good luck with you. Listen idiot. This is easy for you.'

'Do I have to get tattoos? On my neck and face?'

Miguel thumped his leg again, but didn't say anything.

III

Mamá made turkey and frijoles panuchos for them on Sunday, mostly because her husband preferred cochinita pibil – she had marinated the pork, it was in a bowl under a cloth in the kitchen and Ramón had seen the achiote peelings in the trash, but panuchos was what had arrived at the table. In silence Pedro forked cabbage and avocado into his mouth, his head low and his elbows resting on the plastic tablecloth. It had tiny rosebuds all over it; in the centre of the table was a single plastic rose in a green vase, chaperoned by a cluster of sweating Coke bottles that Pedro had brought with him. Ramón had not yet heard if he would be going back to the dive. He inspected his shin where he had been kicked during football that morning. It oozed spots of blood if he squeezed it hard enough. He grabbed a Coke and leant his chair back on one leg so he could see the TV, which was showing one of the telenovelas that his sisters love so much. Ramón had not followed this one much recently because of being away with Papá but Maria Fernanda had filled him in while they were laying the table together.

Ramón looked around the table. Mamá looked tired. She stared in fury at her husband, ignoring her food; out of habit she held her cutlery in a way that displayed her enormously long and decorated nails; they had not spoken a word to each other. The sisters on the other hand, had not stopped talking. They leant their full chests into the table, eating and nattering constantly and pointed with their cutlery at whoever they were talking to, not like the Germans who hardly spoke when they ate.

Ramón cleared the table with Maria Fernanda, glancing at Papá who still had not said anything to him. He chewed his lip and his eyes slid towards his mother. If he couldn't go back on the dive he would have to help with the stupid market stall. Women's work. He had the package from Miguel, which he needed to hide and this was troubling him; it was a heavy brick, tightly wrapped in some sort of plastic canvas and bound with duct tape to make it waterproof. Ramón had temporarily hidden it behind his small pile of school books but it was not safe there. There was nowhere in this house to hide anything. His mother dusted his books and looked through them, so proud, even though her own reading was not so good. The sisters did the laundry and looked after the chickens. No hiding places there. Nothing was his.

His father scraped his chair back, and nodded to Ramón. Get in the truck. Ramón looked at his mother, who couldn't look at him because she was giving her husband the most furious stare she could manage, eyes flat, chin jutting, her hand with its jewelled nails across the base of her neck. The clucking sisters were quiet. Ramón ran, brushing past his mother on the way; he had to get the parcel before his father reached the truck.

IV

They slept in the truck but the divers weren't allowed to know that. Ramón's head was in his father's lap but he couldn't sleep. Papá did not snore in a regular way but occasionally let out breathless snorts and sat upright, which made Ramón jerk awake. Andrés slept in the minibus and Ramón thought it would be better if they all slept there; at least they would each have had a seat to stretch out on. Papá said he didn't trust Andrés not to slit their throats in the night so that cheap cabrón Ernesto could take his business.

Ramón kept his head still so as not to wake Papá, but reached into his shorts pocket to find his penknife – a gift from tiá Magda, which neither parent admitted he had. He flipped through the tools. A small knife, a tiny screwdriver, a bottle opener, and a corkscrew; he ran his finger up and down the spiral, testing the point on his tongue. Ramón opened the little knife and pushed it into his palm until he drew blood. The knife was not sharp enough and he had to push hard for it to break the skin. He sucked the brown red drops and thought about the package. It was under the seat in the truck cabin where they were lying. He knew what it was. Ramón had seen Zetas caches on the TV news many times before. What if the stupid package bumped around when his father was driving so that his father had to look under the seat?

V

Monday morning meant they were back at the deep cave with the golden turquoise beam of sunlight. They went early again. Ramón had to help his father bring the equipment down to the platform this time; Andrés had found an old climbing harness, which he strapped round the bulky items to lower them down the shaft. Ramón waited at the bottom with his father to untie the rope.

'Better stand back because that old fool probably can't tie a good knot,' warned Pedro. Ramón kept his eyes on the stairs. The water seemed particularly dark today. Brooding. Fuck this, he muttered when his father had moved across the platform. What's so special about this fucking cave? Apart from that it's so difficult to get to. Three thousand cenotes and Horst, cabrón, he wants this one.

Ramón had seen the maps, with the rock profiles of the caves. He knew that this one had the important connecting branches to the other cave systems. He decided he wouldn't look at the turquoise beam of light today, or at the water. He would do his work. He had his basket of towels for the divers and when the equipment was down, he had to climb back up the ladder and clean off the steps once more. Miguel's package was at the bottom of the basket under the towels. The divers shouldn't need them until he was back down, ready to hand them out and there should be no need for Papá to look through the towels. Ramón kept his eyes fixed on each step as he wiped it, concentrated on finding a dry part of the rag to use. He didn't look at Serena's perfect feet coming down after him, her pale toes gripping the steps. She was blocking out the light and wanted to come down faster than he would let her.

'It's still slippery,' he mumbled, not looking up.

When they were all down, Ramón got the divers' lights out of the crate and lined them up with their battery canisters and cables. Horst would want to check everything himself. Each diver would have two lights as well as two nitrox tanks. Ramón kept his eyes on the cables, which he had to curl in loose rings so they didn't get kinks in them. Another of his important jobs. Serena put her suit on, covering her white hair, which she whipped into a bun with a quick turn of her wrist and tucked into the black neoprene hood.

When the divers had disappeared below the surface, Pedro heaved himself up the ladder again to see what Andrés was up to, and to smoke in the open air. Ramón had to stay down at the bottom and call up to him when the divers came back. That was fine by him. He lugged the towel basket over to his rock at the back of the platform. It was dark there; he was alone. He looked over to the beam of turquoise gold and said a quick prayer to the Our Lady of the Candelaria, hoping that was the right thing to do. Maybe such prayers would make the goddess angrier with him?

Ramón had been thinking about the package ever since Miguel had given it to him. He had been told more would come and they would all be waterproof, canvas boat bags covered in duct tape. They used to hide them under the bottom of boats but that didn't work anymore so they needed to find new places. Ramón was supposed to leave this stuff everywhere he went on these days out with the divers. He had to remember all the hiding places without writing any down. Miguel said this made Ramón important. Worth a lot of money.

Ramón settled down to wait on his rock, his head against the limestone wall. One arm lay across the sisal basket, the other one snaked silently into it, reached under the towels and touched the package. It was cool. He could feel the fibres of the duct tape under his fingers. He took hold of one corner and slowly withdrew the package bit by bit, looking under his lashes at the water of the lake. It rippled slightly. He didn't have long. As he withdrew the package, the weight of it bent the rim of the bag onto his knees. Soon Ramón could see the white beams of the diver's HID lights over at the back of the lake. They were switched off one after the other as the four of them entered the main cave. Papá should come down and be there when they surfaced.

The package was heavier and more slippery than Ramón had expected. He needed to stand up and call Papá but he had to hide this slippery brick before the divers came; his hand was shaking and in his rush Ramón's fingers missed their hold, the package fell from his knee and slid down the side of the platform through a gap by the cave wall. There was a gentle splash, as if a fish had jumped. Then silence. The water was not deep there, but they would have to pull the platform up to get it. That was not good. The first one and he'd screwed up. He tried to peer between the slats and down the side of the platform, as he got up to take the towels to the divers but he couldn't see any silver tape – it must be under the water and had slipped away into the dark.

There was a BBQ supper on at the motel that night. Pedro and the Germans had taken over one end of the restaurant where two fat men sweated under sombreros and played guitar for the guests. Andrés, shirt unbuttoned, leant on the railings picking his teeth, flicking his Zippo lighter open and shut. The divers were pleased with their progress, especially Horst, who clinked beer bottles with Pedro and Andrés. Plates of sweet pork ribs and burgers were handed round and even Serena was chatty. She ruffled Ramón's hair, like he was a kid.

Magda Estrellita came to the camp for the evening and brought her two daughters, Borita and Linda. They clung to their mother, shyly kicking their patent shoes in the dust and pulling at their hair, which she had braided and tied off with strawberry baubles. As his cousins, the little girls were

Ramón's responsibility for the evening and he would have to sit with them at the other end of the long table, away from the adults. They stood together, bellies sticking out, chins on their chest. They looked at his feet and grinned at each other. Ramón suspected that once they had got used to the new people, when they thought the adults were not looking, they would try to kiss him, like at Easter. Their tactic was for one of them to run past him as fast as possible and with a glancing touch of wet lips, kiss the back of his hand, or his neck, whatever they could reach, then run off to find the other, squealing with feigned embarrassment. The thought that Serena might see them do that made him squirm in his chair. He scowled at the girls. They nudged each other and looked pleased.

Magda had brought Ramón a magazine from Tulúm where she was a guide. It had pictures of Mayan glyphs on the front and a view of the sea. She had placed it on the table in front of him and was leaning over the back of his chair, turning the pages for him.

'Everybody has to work, Ramón, but you have to read, every day,' she told him. He liked tiá Magda. She put her arms round his neck and kissed his cheek. 'Eh, Ramóncito?' He knew she liked him too. She was small, her body tight. Her breasts were high even though she was not much younger than his mother. She was supposed to have met Rosa when they were young and fierce instead of just angry. Magda had introduced Rosa to her brother, Pedro, who worked as a mechanic in those days and within a year Monserratte was born. Ramón couldn't imagine his mother pert and agile like this little woman whose face smoothed into a relaxed smile when she spoke to foreigners. Rosa was even rude to her customers.

The burgers were burnt on the outside with a blackened crust, grey pink on the inside. They weren't spiced properly because of the foreigners, but Ramón ate his anyway. Linda and Borita didn't want their food. They threw little pieces of meat over the restaurant handrail to a skinny white dog with a long tail.

The cook at the BBQ was a sallow man in a black and white chequered apron, who Ramón hadn't noticed before. He re-tied his headscarf as Ramón came to the counter for another burger and looked at Ramón with such intensity that it scared him a little. He scurried back to the table with his plate empty. He might ask Miguel about this man. Magda had also noticed the cook. She put her hand on her hip and gave him a flat stare, which the cook returned. A minute later he ambled over, wiping his hands on his apron and hissing at the dog. He put his knuckles on the table and leant across to Ramón:

'They'll make him sick,' he said in a low voice, nodding towards the dog.

Ramón stared at his plate; the little girls were quiet. Magda hissed at his back, smoothing down the crumpled shirt material on Ramón's shoulders. She continued to mutter and glare at him until he was behind his grill again. Pedro looked at the cook, who jutted his chin like a shrug and flipped a row of burgers. The Germans didn't seem to have noticed anything, except Horst who leaned over to Pedro.

'Trouble?'

'Temperamental cook,' said Pedro, glancing at his sister. She had returned to the Tulúm magazine and showed Ramón a picture of the coral reef defending the ancient settlement.

'You have to know where the gap is so you can get through. Just like in the old days they light a torch on the beach opposite the place, so the sailors can find the way in,' she told him, loud enough for the Germans to hear.

The divers called Magda Estrellita over to them and she explained how it could be done. Tonight would be possible. The guards allow a party a couple of times a year. For money. Quite a lot of money, because it's secret. The ruins look beautiful in the firelight and you have to come via the sea because the public can't know and you don't want to be seen coming along the road there at night. The boat has to be paid for. The sailor will be skilled and trustworthy, a cousin of the guards. The booze and the entertainment are supplied by the guards as well. You have to pay them in advance. They make bonfires, which they dismantle first thing in the morning. Only sympathetic guests are invited because nobody can find out.

'What do the police do if they find out?' asked Horst.

'They know about it but the guards pay them to ignore it. If they catch you on the road, they will charge you a large bribe to keep quiet. Trust me. It's better this way,' she said with a wink.

Ramón had seen this before – the combination of an illicit party and an ancient monument was worth being ripped off for. The Germans were in. Pedro would drive them to the boat and Andrés could take a night off.

Magda Estrellita sprayed the little girls with insect repellent and then did Ramón. Look after them, she said. Be good Rita and Linny. She waggled her finger at her daughters but they ignored her; they were following a column of sugar ants and arguing about which direction they had come from. Magda and Pedro carried a cold-box full of beers over to the minibus. She climbed in and handed out bottles to the Germans who were already seated. Pedro slid the door shut and Ramón watched the red lights of the minibus recede along the motel drive.

Ramón wondered what to do next. The cook had taken his triangular headscarf off and was scraping down the BBQ, still scowling. Other guests had moved over to the bar at the far end of the restaurant. Borita and Linda were outside the restaurant hut, following ants along the railings, the dog watching them with its tongue hanging out of the side of its mouth.

On the other side of the courtyard Gustavo was alone in the reception hut. 'Vámonos,' said Ramón quietly to the girls. They looked at him for a second and then got back to the ants.

'Eh, come on, I want to go to the pool tables.' Ramón glanced at the cook.

'We don't like pool.'

'There is TV there...'

'We don't like TV.'

'I have a Coke for you. I won't tell your Mamá.'

'We had Coke.'

'OK. OK. Hey – I will tell you a scary story I know. A crazy crazy one.'

Now he had their attention. They scampered after him, shouting his name. The dog decided not to follow and ambled back to the cook who threw him some charred BBQ scrapings. At the reception hut, it turned out Gustavo was expecting them. He pointed at three plastic chairs set up in front of the TV and gave them all a Coke. You have to wait here, he said. Ramón shoved his hands into his pockets. Borita and Linda became shy again. Gustavo lit a cigarette, ignoring them, then he put cartoons on the TV and the girls settled down to watch. He offered Ramón a cigarette, a dented thing which Ramón took and put behind his ear, feeling the inevitable cuff of his mother's hand round the back of his head. He would save it for when he next played football at home.

Borita and Linda soon remembered Ramón's promise. Come on Ramóncito, you promised. Oh. You promised. A real scary one. We'll tell tío Pedro about the cigarette. Mamá will tell tía Rosa. Oh. Come on. Tell it to us. Ohhh.

Ramón didn't know any stories. This was not turning out well. He started to think, picking at the new hole in his shorts; before long his mouth was telling a story his brain hadn't heard before.

'There is the old and jealous goddess of the water,' he said. 'Deep, deep in the sacred wells of our land, she is still there, waiting and watching. She is very important because our land has no rivers. Not one. She is being dishonoured every day by her people who pee in the water of the cenotes, leave their trash and pry into her secret places. She is sold for money every day to tourists, like a common whore. But she is stronger than you think and she has a long memory. She gets angrier every day. She is strict and she demands that we return to the old ways or she will have her revenge – there must be sacrifice. Children will be given to the goddess again, like at Chichen Itza. It's the tradition. They drug them and throw them into the pool where they sink down, down to the bottom. It has always been our way. Precious things must be sacrificed – and nothing is more precious than the little children.'

'Not girls. It's boys they do. Isn't it Ramón?' Eyes wide, Borita and Linda agreed that it wouldn't be the girls.

'Anyway, if you don't go there, nothing can happen. Can it?' Linda's face folded and her bottom lip stuck out. Tears welled up and dotted her cheeks. Borita's mouth turned down and she looked at the TV. Ramón threw a look at Gustavo who was on his cell; he turned the TV volume up and heaved Linda onto his lap so they could watch the cartoons again. Soon Linda was quiet. A little snuffle escaped from time to time between the two fingers she sucked to fall asleep.

Later in the night, Ramón heard barking and voices whispering. Linda was peeled off him, her warm imprint replaced instantly by cool night air. Gustavo was nowhere to be seen and someone had turned off the TV. Ramón felt himself carried over to the truck and laid on the seat. The door shut. Pedro took a blanket to roll himself in and climbed onto the back of the truck. In the night, some noise or other woke Ramón. He sat bolt upright and felt under the seat – there was another parcel there. He groaned and flopped back down to sleep.

Later, he wondered about that parcel. Did Miguel sneak into the camp in the night and put a new package there without telling him? Had the cook put it there? Magda? Was Magda up to her old trouble? Rosa must never know.

The cave diving schedule was interrupted the next day because the divers were too tired and hung-over to dive safely. A late morning trip to an open cenote was planned instead, where they could snorkel and sunbathe and with less equipment, they could all get in the minibus. Ramón did not often travel with aircon and he found it too cold. Magda and the girls were keen for a swim, especially if Ramón was coming too, but he still didn't have any swimmers.

The cenote Pedro had chosen was a favourite with tourists but also with local Mexicans who came as families for a day out, the women wearing their brightly coloured swimming costumes and layers of jeweller so that in the water they glittered more than the fish, which were dull. Many of them swam in full makeup with big red lips and stood around eating chicharrón and tortilla chips when they came out of the water, their bellies hanging over their thighs. They laughed and shouted across the pool to each other. Sometimes the platform was heaving with people damp and writhing for position, waiting to get up the stairs and shuffling to the side to let others come down, bodies like plump brown eels together, slimy to the touch and jostling for position. They roiled off the platform and into the water, screeching and laughing and even some of the men wore armbands or life jackets, unashamed, like little children.

At least his foreigners were calm and respectful of the cenotes. But the foreigners didn't own them. They didn't come in the same way as the Mexican families – the cenotes were part of Yucatán culture. Even though they loved them, Ramón had to admit the people were ruining them. They should all go and leave them as they were. They should all get out, even the Mexicans. Go to the beach. Only priests should be allowed to go to the cenotes, and villagers for water, when they didn't have other supplies. People from Cancún, or other towns should stay away.

Ramón looked around. The cenote was wider at the top than many because the roof had collapsed in a time before local memory, leaving the pool almost completely open to the sky. It had steps that curved round the side of the wall descending to the cave floor. Small fish zipped across the white limestone powder on the bottom of the pool, darting in threes and fours through the turquoise water. For once there was plenty of vegetation, the cracks in the rocks were full of waving ferns and grasses. Despite the popularity of the place, all the shrieking and splashing, the cenote contained a special fish that the divers wanted to see, so they had brought their cameras and snorkelling gear but no tanks or scooters. A terrapin bobbed its head out of the water and clung to the cave wall.

Ramón walked slowly down the steps, guarding his basket, the package hidden beneath the towels. A little bridge led across the water to a large flattened rock in the middle of the lake with two benches on it; several families of Mexicans had taken over this area, talking at the top of their voices and passing fizzy drinks and bags of chips to each other. One family seemed to consist entirely of shrill teenaged girls with puppy fat breasts. Ramón ignored them although the volume of noise escalated all the time. He watched the Germans descend regally into this chaos, to slip their long pale limbs into the water hardly making a ripple, leaving their clothes and books with Ramón. Pedro and Andrés hung over the railing up at ground level, smoking and looking down at the scene.

Borita and Linda wanted Ramón to come into the water. They had bright orange arm bands on and matching swimsuits, they looked like little satsumas bobbing in the water. They paddled over to him and Borita hefted herself onto the side. She wrapped her hand around his ankle and pulled at it.

'Come on Ramóncito. You promised.'

'I am working,' he hissed at the girls, shaking his leg free. Serena hadn't noticed. Magda Estrellita waded across and hooked the girls' arms over an inflatable ring with a duck's head which she swirled round and round in the water for them.

Ramón searched the walls of the cave. He was looking for a deep nook about head height, with a plant sticking out of it. He had to hide this package safely, and soon; they wouldn't be staying here for long. Despite all the greenery, the cave looked unpromising. Too busy. He shuffled the bag round the edge of the water with his feet, trying not to be obvious in his search. Serena already thought he was weird and Horst just stared all the time.

About half way round from the bottom of the steps and behind a large boulder there was a gap that had possibilities. It was a little lower than he had hoped for. Maybe the package wouldn't have to stay there too long. Anyway, it would have to do. He shuffled toward it with his bag of towels, all the time watching to see who was looking.

Soon Ramón was standing by the side of a small cleft about a metre up which had a fern growing down from it. He could see that behind there was a gap but it looked too small; he poked about with his penknife, deftly widening the gap behind the plant. A quick check over his shoulder told him nobody was interested in him; he bent down to his towel bag, grabbed a towel and draped it over his shoulder, like a Conquistador's cape. He had the heavy package in his right hand under the towel, his left hand reached for his nose and scratched. He feigned a cough and shoved the parcel backwards into the niche, behind the fern. Soon he'd get a cell phone of his own.

Ramón looked around. He stroked the fern around the indentation and started to shuffle back towards the steps. He looked up. His father and Andrés were following him with their eyes. They were no longer talking, although Andrés was pointing at him with his cigarette. Magda was still in the water, Borita clinging to her back, Linda lying across her arms, learning to float; she gave Ramón a smile and turned back to her children. Fuck. Fuck. Everybody knows. I will be dead meat and so will Miguel. Ramón's legs felt weak. He heard a shout – Hey, Ramón! He turned too quickly and nearly misplaced his footing. Steadying himself against the wall of the cave, Ramón looked across the pool. It was only the Germans – they had seen enough and wanted to get out. Ramón must bring the towels to the central rock platform.

Ramón picked his way across the rickety bridge, balancing carefully with the sisal basket held out in front of him. He couldn't see his feet so he made his way by tapping his toes in front of himself before putting his weight on each foot. It took concentration, especially since he was trying not to think about the package in its niche. Just as Ramón reached the safety of the central platform, a turmoil of teenage girls burst around him, screeching and pushing, chasing each other across the bridge. There were flailing limbs, teeth, flicking wet hair and chubby wet bottoms. He wobbled. He put his front foot down, his head jutted forward, his backside went out as counterbalance. He hung onto his basket, wobbled again but steadied himself – just as one last wet mound of blubber battled past him onto the bridge screeching in his ear like a wounded turkey. Pedro had started down the stairs before his son was in the water.

The whole cenote exploded with hilarity. Andrés wiped tears from his eyes. The teenage girls shrieked and giggled, huddling together. Pedro was not laughing. Magda waded towards Ramón, lifted her daughters onto the flat island rock and helped Ramón to retrieve the towels from the pool. He tried to hide a sob as the heavy material flopped into muddy puddles. Furious, Pedro collected the sisal bag, the ruined paperbacks, wet clothes and towels. Ramón climbed out and tried to drag more sodden towels over to the bench, out of the mud. Pedro dumped the bag at Ramón's feet. He grabbed Ramón by the shoulder and yanked him towards him, but Horst spoke in his loud and heavily accented Spanish. 'It vas not his fault. No problem. Leave him.'

Pedro was silent, his eyes fixed on Horst. So was Ramón. Magda raised her eyebrows with a flicker and turned back to her daughters. All the Mexicans were silent. Pedro's arm began to vibrate on Ramón's shoulder. He looked down at his own feet. His client had unaccountably, unforgivably interfered with his family authority.

Ramón began to cry. Sorry, Papá, sorry. He squirmed out of his father's grip and ran to the stairs. The noise level resumed and Pedro gathered up the soaking towels. He stomped up the wooden staircase with them in his arms.

VI

The next day Pedro brought them to the Gran Cenote by Tulúm, another popular location. The divers wanted to test some new lights, but Ramón couldn't care less; he had other work now. He had hidden six packages in the last week and would surely get paid soon.

Ramón looked around at all the people and thought this one was too busy to hide anything. They had been to cenotes all over the state and mostly he had found very good places, where nobody would look. Papá hadn't noticed, or if he had, he hadn't said anything. The mystery was how the packages were arriving. Miguel was not often there, but the cook, Magda and Andrés were all possibilities, although nobody said anything or even hinted to him when he hung around like a dog looking for scraps. He wanted people to know he was trusted, even if he didn't yet know who by. He wanted Miguel to bring some money for him. He wanted his own cell phone. Everybody in the world had a cell phone except him. Ramón knew what was in the packages. There was another one under the car seat, which had been there for a whole day and he didn't want to think about that. He was also beginning to forget exactly where the packages were, the hiding places getting mixed up in his mind. Ramón looked along a covered tunnel leading away from the main pool. He felt his heart pounding. Swallows zinged in and out of the low overhang, where they had made upside down volcanoes of spit and mud for nests.

A hand was on his shoulder.

'Ramón!'

He spun around and saw Miguel.

'Oh, Miguel. I'm glad you're here because…'

'OK, come.' Miguel's eyes were shining, black and tiny. His cheeks were more sallow and sunken than before, his acne standing out more red.

'I can't leave the towels.' Ramón looked around for Pedro and Horst.

'Let them get their own fucking towels, idiot, we have to go.'

'Where? Not for long?' Ramón followed his brother up the stairs, hoping he wouldn't be missed. 'Miguel, there will be trouble for Papá if I am not there.' They crossed the parking lot to the red sports car, Miguel's only possession.

'Shut up, idiot. Get in. You are not so important, that he can't manage without you, towel boy.' He opened the door and slammed it hard after Ramón. The car pulled backwards in an arc that sprayed stones and dust, then with a jolt that nearly made Ramón bang his head on the dash, Miguel threw the car forward into the empty space next to Pedro's Nissan truck and slammed the brakes.

'What the fuck, Miguel.'

'I need you to do something for me.' Miguel's hand shook a little as he lit the cigarette from behind his ear. Ramón patted down his pockets, found his precious cigarette, smoothed out the wrinkles and put it behind his ear, on the left so Miguel could see. Miguel thumped Ramón's thigh with his fist.

'It's very important. Idiot.'

'What Miguel? I have hidden everything. Like you said.'

Miguel didn't reply but nodded sideways once or twice as if he had an ant in his ear.

'Where were you? I kept finding packages. But I didn't see you.'

'Shut up, idiot. I have something else for you to hide. Something important. Bigger. We must get it into the truck while Papá is with the tourists.'

'Where will I hide something big?'

'You will have to work it out. Andrés will help.'

'Andrés?'

'He will be paid.'

'Why doesn't he hide the packages instead of me? Look Miguel, I want my money. I want to buy a cell...'

'Shut it. You do what you are told. Andrés has to stay with the cars. He isn't in the holes like you. Anyway – he's not so reliable. Idiot.'

Ramón was not sure what to make of this. He hung his arm out of the window and beat a tune on the door.

'Another thing,' said Miguel. 'I need some of the packages. Maybe four.'

'We won't be going back for another week to most of them. Maybe longer.'

'We'll go now, you and me. Where are the nearest ones?'
Miguel looked at Ramón, made loose circular motions with his hand. 'All near to this highway, no?'

'Miguel. There is one in the truck.'

'What?'

'I haven't hidden it yet. I was going to…'

'Je-sus. Get it!'

Miguel looked around to see who was watching the cars in the parking lot. Andrés was by the minibus, making a call and smoking, kicking dirt into small clouds. He couldn't see anyone else. 'Vámonos. We'll risk it.

They clambered into the truck cabin. It smelled of Papá's sweat. Miguel exhaled deeply, rested his head on the back of the seat, closed his eyes and for a minute seemed to relax. With a snap of his neck he jerked himself awake.

'Come on. Where is it, Ramón?' he barked, feeling under the seat.

Ramón reached under his feet and passed the silver package to his brother. He kept his eyes on his knees, picked the seam of his shorts. Miguel grunted but seemed calmer.

'Where's the next one? The nearest? We have to go.'

'I can't leave – Papá will kill me. He'll be in trouble.'

'Idiot.'

'The dive will get messed up.'

'So? Fuck them.'

'They will look for me.'

Miguel considered this. 'I will text Papá. Later.'

'He will be mad with you, Miguel.'

'There are worse things. First, I'm gonna fix the truck.'

Covering the package with a spare towel, Miguel got out and tossed the bundle into the footwell of the SP2. From the Nissan cabin, Ramón could see that the towel had fallen right off again and the whole block covered in duct tape was visible. A realisation came to him. Miguel is careless. He is also more frightened than me.

The big package for Ramón was in the trunk of the SP2. Leaning forward, Miguel glanced under his arm to survey the parking lot again. He lifted a Nike sports bag out, and clutching it to one armpit, got back into the dive truck cabin hiding his actions with the door. He passed it to Ramón, who held it just long enough to know what was in it, the heavy metallic shapes clearly recognisable. Three guns. Handguns. So, now it *is* guns, he thought.

'Eh, Mano?' said Miguel. With a nod and flick of his eyebrows he had twitched the bag away from Ramón and was now outside, under the truck where Ramón could hear the ripping of duct tape and felt the floorboard of the truck shift as Miguel fixed the bag to the underside of the truck.

Then he was back in the cabin brushing his hands together to dust them off. 'You got your little knife, right?' he said.

'Yes, Miguel.'

'Cos it won't come off easy. Don't want it knocked off by Papá's lousy driving.'

'OK, Miguel.'

'Let's go. Get in.' Miguel nodded at his own car; Ramón got out of the truck and looked all over the parking lot for Papá. Andrés was still ignoring them. He lowered himself into the passenger seat, trying not to touch the silver brick lying on the floor then he flicked the towel over it with his foot.

The brothers were quiet for a moment. Miguel turned the key in the ignition, put his arm round the back of Ramón's seat and looked out the back window.

'Is this what they do at the *hotel*, Miguel?'

'Shut the fuck up, idiot.' Miguel reversed out of the parking lot at speed, a cigarette dangling from his lip and his elbow out the window.

'Text Papá.'

'I will.'

*

Half an hour later, they were at the nearest cenote. Miguel knew most of the ones around Highway 307, the main route that Pedro used. Ramón took him down the ladder and showed him where to look, but there were too many people. Miguel would come back later.

'Good job, little brother' he said and Ramón began to relax. They visited three more cenotes; Ramón remembered where everything was and they brought two more packages away.

'Mamá will kill you. Or Papá will,' Ramón said to his brother.

They were leaning over a railing above an open Cenote. Miguel had bought Ramón a blue coloured sorbet but he wasn't allowed it in the precious car.

'They won't. '

'They will.' Ramón was sure his mother would find out and her fury would rock the whole peninsula.

'You don't know anything about them. Or Magda. Let's go.'

On the way back to Papá, Miguel said 'Just keep your mouth shut. OK?'

'O-kay Miguel. I'm not a kid.'

'They don't want to talk about it, you know.'

'OK.' Ramón studied his tongue in the side mirror. It was an interesting purple colour and tasted of gum.

Miguel swung his car into the parking lot with a flourish. He pulled up next to the diving truck again and lit another cigarette. Instantly their father was there. He ripped open the car door and dragged Miguel out by the shirt front.

'What have you done?'

Serena came running over and calling over her shoulder to her colleagues.

'Where? Why?' Miguel stared his father out.

Pedro sucked his breath and struck Miguel across the face with the back of his hand sending spit flying to the ground. A second later he swung a punch that caught his father on the cheek. Stunned, Pedro sat down onto the ground like a baby. 'Oh!' Serena clamped her hand over her mouth. Horst and two other divers came running up to them. Ramón was so embarrassed he wanted to cry.

'I'll help you, Papá.' He got his hand under Pedro's arm and tried to lift his father off the floor.

'Get away!'

Ramón couldn't stop the tears which streamed down his face. Miguel got back in his car and drove away. He pointed his finger at Ramón as he left, to remind him about the parcel under the truck. He looked in the rear view mirror and was gone with a squeal of tyres and then usual spray of stones.

By now a group of divers had come over to the truck. Ramón wiped his face with the heel of his palm, and then wiped his hand on his shorts. Horst stepped forward. Without hesitation, he reached his huge hand down to Pedro. Pedro touched his fingers to a red welt swelling on his cheekbone. He looked at the gravel. Eventually he lifted his eyes to look at the massive grey man, took the hand and allowed himself to be helped up.

'I alzo hef a son,' said the German in a low voice. 'Aah – I hed a son. He is gone, long time now I don't see him.' They stood together for a moment; then Horst turned away.

Serena was furious. She looked at Ramón and his father like they were rats that had run across her plate. With a swirl of white hair, she turned her back on them and marched off to her cabin.

When the others had gone, Pedro slapped Ramón hard on the cheek. 'Where were you? We have been looking for you for two hours. We have searched the water and the bush here. Where the fuck have you been?'

'Miguel came. He said he would text you. '

'Where is Andrés? Was he with you?'

'No. I don't know. He was by the minibus when we left.'

With a stream of the most elaborate obscenities Ramón had ever heard his father use, Pedro walked back to the divers, leaving Ramón alone. There was nobody to drive the minibus, if Andrés had left.

A few minutes later, Pedro came back.

'Get in the truck. Drink this. I will be back if I can. It will be late.' He passed Ramón a bottle of water and the blanket from the back of the truck. 'If not me, Alfredo will come. The keys are here.' He threw the truck keys onto the seat.

'I mean it – stay in the truck, Ramón.'

'Tío Alfredo? Magda's Alfredo?' Ramón asked, but all he could see was his father's retreating back.

Ramón climbed into the truck cabin. It must be Magda Estrellita's Alfredo. Maybe she would come with him and bring Ramón something to eat. She made good poc chuc. Also good mole tomales, but not as good as Mamá. His stomach gurgled. He knew the divers were going back to the motel for another BBQ but that he had to stay with the truck at the cenote. Papá had to make everything cool with the Germans.

The cenote where Ramón waited alone in the truck was down a dirt track about five kilometres off Highway 307, not far from La Esperanza. IParked under trees, the vehicle was tucked in amongst the thick vegetation in a small bay close to the track. Ramón leaned sideways, his head on the seat. Then he lifted his feet up onto the seat. Then he curled into a ball and pulled the blanket over his head. The birds were getting louder and seemed nearer. Nobody knows I am here, he thought. Probably I'll just be here in the dark, with the noises, the calling and the rustling in the bushes, until Alfredo comes. That could be late. Magda's house is maybe an hour away from here? Who knows where Alfredo is working? He might be collecting from the airport tonight. He won't bring that fancy taxi out here. Maybe he'll go home and get Magda's car. If he does that, she might put tomales in a bag for him to bring to me.

Ramón searched the compartment and the pockets of the doors looking for sweets and gum. Nothing, only wrappers. The keys were there, so he could put the radio on, or the lights, but that might attract attention and maybe it'd be better to stay quiet, let nobody know. There was a torch. He got it out and shone it onto his palm. It was small but powerful. Good. It was getting darker and there were no lights; the sky still too pale for stars. Something shouted 'yak, yak, yak, yak' close to the truck. He wound up the windows, checking they were up as tight as they would go. A thin branch scratched the windscreen making a scraping noise that sounded like it was inside the cabin. He rooted around in the door compartment for a mosquito coil, but couldn't find one. No matches anyway. Ramón got his penknife out of his pocket and started going through the tools in strict rotation. See, if I had a cell phone of my own, I could text Mamá and tell her where I am. Except, I don't know where this is exactly. I don't think Papá should leave me here like this with the truck and the equipment to guard, because – I'm only a kid. She would tell him. I could have texted Papá myself and let him know Miguel had come, so they wouldn't all be furious because they'd been looking for me all afternoon. Maybe they forgot the towels down in the cenote. What about Serena's hair towels? Nobody said what happened to the towels. Do they know where to get the clean ones at the motel in the morning? They need me. They will come back for me. Papá loves me, the bastard, he is a fuck but Mamá will really kill him if anything happens to me. He's angry because we have a big day tomorrow when they will film the exploration. Tomorrow they want to take all the cameras and equipment down and now Andrés has disappeared. Papá might have to ask his enemy, cabrón Ernesto, for help. That would kill him, if he had to do that, it really would. Ramón could see Papá on his cell to Ernesto asking for help, then clutching his heart with his hand, his shirt twisting in his fist and then he flings his body backwards, his mouth wide, eyes turn up to the sky. Killed by Ramón and Miguel, the bad sons who made their father ask his enemy for help.

I will give him my money. Never mind about the cell. When Miguel pays me, I will give Papá my money, for the family, and I will tell Miguel to give his money to Papá too, or to Mamá if they are still not talking and it will be for the good of the family and we won't have to defile the cenotes anymore. We can go away because I can hear the goddess calling me and she is angry with me too. I feel the spirits swirling in the water, faster and faster, circling me. It is my family's fault that the foreigners are here. We have defiled the waters. We are responsible. I have pissed in them. Everybody gets into the cold lakes and immediately pisses in the water. The goddess is being pissed on. Ramón banged his head on the back of the truck hard, once, twice. *OK little one, OK.* He heard the whisper. *It will be OK. You know what to do.*

Ramón opened the door of the truck a tiny crack and listened. Where were the noises from the jungle? Was something coming? A jaguar? He snapped the door shut and looked through the windscreen. It was dark now. The sky had a yellow cast towards Cancún from the city lights, but there were stars overhead, high and bright; many more the longer you looked. Still, no other lights except for a little moonlight. Sometimes people went hunting in the jungle at night. But they had dogs. And bows. A massive dog might come bounding out of the bushes. The hunter might help, or might not. *Don't worry about any dogs little one; everything will be OK.*

Twenty minutes later Ramón had made up his mind. He needed protection. Who knew what was out there? He slithered over to the driver's seat and inched the door open. The dirt path looked pale grey in the moonlight, narrowing into the distance. He had his penknife in his hand and facing the door, he rolled his hips down until his toes curl over the edge of the step. Very slowly, he put both feet on the floor and allowed his weight to flow into them as he moved his body away from the seat. He grabbed the torch and shuffled along the side of the truck. The keys were in his pocket. Nobody was going to leap out of the jungle and drive off with the truck. He was too smart for that.

Ramón slid further along the side of the truck, keeping his back in contact with it, making sure to leave the door open a crack. Holding his breath he squatted to feel under the truck, flashing the torch into the dark recess before he put his hand under there – he knew where Miguel had put the bag of guns. When he reached the right place, he lowered himself to lie on the ground. He whistled between his teeth, murmuring 'Miguel, Miguel' to himself. He hoped a snake would not come. He reached up to the package which he felt all over, trying to keep the back of his head off the ground. 'Miguel. Miguel. Miguel.' He could cut it away from the truck with his penknife, and separate the guns. Miguel wouldn't know till too late, but he couldn't hide all of the guns together anyway – the package would be too big for that. Miguel should have thought of that. The bag dropped into his hands with a small clink. Ramón froze. Had he heard the crunch of footsteps along the track? He wanted to shine his torch to see what it was. It might just be an animal. It could be a man. He didn't know what would be worse. A prayer came into his head, to Our Lady of the Candelaria. He started to say the words under his breath but what came out were muttering noises with too much tongue and saliva. It was better to be quiet. Even in your head. He tried to listen again. Stones pressed into his back, they were sticking into his shoulder blades and spine, he wanted to wriggle, to leap out sideways and fly into the truck cabin, slam the door and lock it. He wanted to be somewhere else. He lay as still as he could but his arm was going numb. He decided he couldn't hear anything anymore. He ratcheted his hips and shoulders sideways, centimetre by centimetre like a hunched caterpillar, until his head was out from under the truck. He gripped the bag of guns in one hand, the torch in the other. Nothing seemed to be moving. He whipped himself up and into the truck before anything else could come.

Ramón banged the door locks down and, breathing hard, allowed himself to cry. He pulled the blanket over himself, and let the tears flow. *Don't worry, little one. You are doing well. Everything will be OK.*

The blanket was thick and scratchy and full of burro hairs, which stuck to his sweating skin. He had never been alone this long, or in such a dark place. The Nike bag was between his curled up knees and his chest. He hadn't seen the guns yet. Was it OK for them to get wet or not? Ramón didn't know. He decided to cut up the bag and separate them. He would make everything waterproof with the spare tape that Pedro kept for the dives. Under the blanket, he opened the bag zipper and took out the guns. They looked heavier than they were when he weighed them in his palm. He couldn't tell if they were loaded or not. There were no bullets in the bag. He decided to risk turning on the torch to examine them; the blanket would keep most of the light in.

Ramón turned them over slowly, passed them from hand to hand. The guns were the same type, similar like cousins. One of them had been painted with gold and silver swirls, meant to look like the gold-plate gangster guns on the TV. He shouldn't have touched the guns, Ramón decided. They wear gloves on the TV, because of fingerprints. The tears came again in great heaving waves as Ramón tried to rub off what he could not see, with his sweat-soaked T-shirt.

Later, he thought he'd gut the canvas Nike bag, hoping to produce enough material to cover the guns, which he could then seal with more duct tape. He said to himself, the guns will be wanted again, otherwise why not just dump them all in the sea? He pointed the guns at his head, and looked at himself in the rear view mirror. He pointed a gun out of each side window, one in each hand, shooting policemen and bikers on all sides. He blasted the vegetation to shreds and all the screaming, biting, poisonous animals it could throw at him. He imagined a snarling jaguar leaping out of the trees, landing on the bonnet with heavy claws. He fired both guns, bam, bam, got it between the eyes because he has been a champion shot since he was a little kid, shooting at cans in the desert. The jaguar died mid leap, crashing onto the bonnet, its open jaw plastered against the windscreen.

Ramón poured the last of the water onto his tongue, swilled it around his mouth and looked at his project. The moon was higher and gave enough light to work with, so long as he didn't need to see in detail. Then he used the torch. His knife was almost blunt, but he could sharpen it in the kitchen at home. He had managed to get two of the guns wrapped and bound neatly, although there was not enough bag material left over to wrap the third, the one with the golden swirls painted on it. The packages were bumpy but he was pretty proud of the job he had done. He put the two guns under the seat and pushed the blanket under there too so they wouldn't rattle about.

Ramón looked out of all of the cabin windows. He couldn't see or hear anything out there. He lay on his back and placed the third gun on his belly, fingers tracing the shapes on the handle. Someone had used enamel paint, like nail varnish. Sometimes gangsters put names on guns, carved in scrollwork. This one was silent about its owner. Which were the removable parts? He had seen in films how the cartridge was knocked out, the clips or whatever, to exchange them, but he couldn't get it to come out. Maybe it was loaded and maybe it wasn't. So what good was it to him? He should have had a look at the other ones before he bagged them up, but if he cut them open, he might not have enough tape to seal them up again. He tucked the gun under his thigh and pressed his leg onto it, liking the feel of its corners against his flesh. Alfredo could be here at any moment. No good sleeping now. He ran his finger along the window seal at the top, checked again that the door locks were down, flicked the torch on and off against his palms to check the batteries hadn't died. He leant his head against the seat back, and his eyes started to droop, the night noises became comforting, hypnotic.

He woke with a start to tapping on the driver's window.

'Hey, mano, make room!' Alfredo's voice was rough from smoking and drinking too much. Ramón's heart leapt. He reached for the gun under his leg and recognising Alfredo's face, stopped himself. He slumped his shoulders again, leant over to the door lock and let his uncle into the cab. It was nearly dawn. Ramón felt as though he hadn't slept at all.

'I need to pee,' he said, although he didn't.

'Be quick.'

Ramón scooted his bottom over to the passenger door, pushed it open against the tall bushes on that side and let the gun fall into his palm as he got out. He went round to the back of the truck. He shoved the gun in a pocket and leant his forehead against the tailgate, his teeth chattering. He didn't know what to do about the stupid gun. He put it on the ground and considered leaving it there.

'Come on, Ramón,' Alfredo shouted, sticking his head out the window.

Ramón tried a few different places with the gun. It was bigger than his hand. It was too big to stay hidden in one of his pockets. It would show through the front of his shirt if he hid it in his waistband. He shoved it in the back of his undershorts hoping it would be hidden by the baggy backside of his shorts and let his shirt hang loose over the top.

Alfredo sucked his teeth when Ramón got back in. 'We have to get the tanks refilled and be ready for the day's business in a minute Ramón. We don't have long.' Alfredo revved up the truck and soon they were rattling back along the dirt track to join Highway 307 and meet Pedro at the motel.

VII

Arriving at the turquoise beam cenote, Ramón felt as though he was in a dream. Everything was too loud and too busy; there were too many people there. Papá appeared cheerful enough, not too angry, but that didn't mean anything because the foreigners were there. He was hurrying back and forth, filling the trolley and bringing things over to the top of the cenote stair shaft. Alfredo lowered the bulky equipment down with the rope and harness. One of the divers was stationed at the bottom, untying it all.

Horst, in strident mood for the big day, gave Ramón a stern warning about keeping the towels dry and then patted his head. He told him not to disappear because they wouldn't have time to look for him. Ramón had been entrusted with cleaning the steps again. He spat at the ground and slapped the cloth against his calf. The sun was bright and he couldn't decide whether he was shivering or sweating. He rubbed his eyes with gritty fingers

In the cave, the camera light hurt Ramón's eyes. He blinked all the time. Waves of shivering passed through his whole body, although he didn't feel all that scared any more. He wanted to sleep. But he couldn't. Impossible. He must work well for his father today; he had to prove himself, he couldn't let Papá down again. Knowing the gun would show when he bent to clean the steps, Ramón hid it and moved it to the commando pocket on the side of his shorts. He buttoned down the pocket so it wouldn't fall out, but it was too bulky. He thought it must be visible and he felt it pull against his leg with every movement. It dragged his shorts down on that side. He wished he had bandaged that stupid gun up too and put it in the towel bag, but maybe that wasn't the right thing. People might get their own towels after his screw-up the other day. He should have left it in the truck with the other two. It was Alfredo's fault he hadn't.

Ramón hitched up his shorts and continued to wipe the steps. Nobody had noticed the bulge on the side of his leg. He would never get away with a gun in his pocket if Mamá was here. *She* would have noticed if her son had a gun in his shorts. Papá couldn't care less. Look at Horst nodding at him. Look at Papá licking that bastard ghost giant up the arse. Look at him gazing over at Serena like he'd never seen a woman before, like he didn't know what she was. She was bending over to separate the air hoses for the tanks. She had no hair on her body at all.

Ramón had a metallic taste in his mouth. He was constantly thirsty but couldn't get rid of this dry, brown taste, like the inside of his mouth was rusting. He wanted another drink but didn't dare ask anybody and he couldn't see the cold box. He moved his bag of towels away from the lights and sat on it for a moment.

'Hey! *Pssp* – Ramón!' His father flicked his finger at the boy's chest to make him wake up. They wanted the fins brought down. He had to lay out the dive lights and their batteries as well. There was work.

All morning Ramón ran up and down the ladder with equipment, forcing himself to stay awake. He carried the fins down to the cave. He took the lamps down; then all the batteries. He took the connecting cables and fitted the charged batteries to the lamps. He laid them out on the cave floor, and all the while the whispering continued in his head. *Do it. Come on. They are not to be here. Do it. Come on. Use the knife. I don't want them here.*

Alfredo surprised Ramón by knowing what to do with the equipment.

'Tío, have you worked on the dives before?'

Alfredo sucked his teeth and jutted his chin.

'Where is Andrés, uncle?'

He shrugged. 'Gone.'

'Where?'

'Just gone.'

Horst was jubilant. He had managed to contact the landowner and paid for exclusive use of the cenote for forty-eight hours. Against Pedro's advice, Horst had also paid the local villagers not to bring any tourists for the next two days. Consequently the place was teeming with people. Every time Ramón came back up to the top, there were more of them. There was a guard at the front of the parking lot who was supposed to turn people away but several cars and trucks had parked there anyway and a small group of women selling corn and bags of chicharrón stood in a corner. A pair of burros laden with embroidered textiles waited in the shade, flicking their tails and twitching their ears. It was like the bullring, something was going to happen. Nobody knew what the foreigners wanted the cenote for. Esoteric rites? Nudity? Filming. Filming what? Who knew? Have you heard what they do at those secret parties at Tulúm? Cigarette ends, sweet wrappers and empty drink bottles appeared on the ground. Not much could be seen from the surface, so people amused themselves by smoking, flirting and gossiping. Something would happen eventually.

Ramón could taste too much perfume on the air. With his eyes closed, he heard the goddess in his head, lisping, muttering. It seemed, he thought, that he had always been able to hear her, but she was louder when he was near this cenote; here he heard little else. She was getting impatient. Angry.

Come on Ramón. Come on. Do something. Make them leave.

The crowd got bigger. The buzz of conversation grew louder, people called to each other, to see if they had seen anything, if over there they knew what was happening. No, nothing. What can you see? Nothing yet. Pedro was important. He barked out orders to Ramón and Alfredo. Serena wore a white bathrobe Ramón hadn't seen before, which hung open over her swimsuit. Sweat trickled between her breasts, hung in pearls on her top lip while she stretched her shoulders out. Horst had been at the top of the stairs all morning, coordinating the equipment, ticking things off on lists that he kept in his head. He was wearing canvas shorts, chest bare, the colourless hairs on his chest curling round small bubbles of sweat until they burst, joined together and rolled down to his navel. The goddess hated him oh so much. She wanted him gone. Her voice was loud in Ramón's head. Horst. It was his fault. It was all his idea. When Ramón went up and down the stairs, he felt Horst's eyes on him, felt him draw near, the heat of his enormous body taking all the air. Ramón was still so thirsty. He stood near the top of the ladder his right hand in his pocket gripping the blunt penknife as hard as he could and he stared at Horst, stared until he saw Horst tip forward, falling, falling, falling, colourless head and eyes falling down the open hole where the steps were, and still Ramón at the top, watched him go, bumping into the ladder, banging his face on the steps, trying to stop himself from falling but getting an arm lodged, wrenched out of joint, broken and misshapen and continuing to fall, until with a mighty crack he fell on his face, his neck broken. Serena, weeping, dabbing the blood off his forehead, and trying to manhandle him back up the stairs because he shouldn't be in the cave, dead and putrid, fat and stinking, but she couldn't do it, and so, when she pleads for his help, it is Ramón who has to drive the crane which will lower grabbers down the hole, take hold of Horst's broken body in its powerful and cruel grip, nearly dropping him and mangling him more before finally getting his corpse out of the cenote cave and taking it down the highway borne up high in front as a tribute to the goddess.

But Horst did not fall. He remained tall and virile, legs planted wide, joking with other divers and in complete command, like some cartoon fuck of a space hero. Just needed a cape. Ramón spat into the dirt. He was still thirsty.

Magda Estrellita arrived for the spectacle, with Borita and Linda. They kissed Alfredo when he was next at the top and then the girls scampered off to draw pictures in the dirt with a little crowd of other children that had appeared. They waved at Ramón and giggled. Ramón had no time to wave back. He was working.

Some of the locals wanted photos with Horst. Two girls in bright makeup took snaps of him from a distance with their cell phones, but didn't dare to talk to him. Ramón thought how easy it would be to hook a cable round his foot and trip him down the hole. Arrogant bastard. He didn't even know who the goddess was.

The gun chaffed at Ramón's skin with its constant banging against his leg. He had started limping to stop it swinging around so much. He went back down the steps to clean them for the third time since early morning. The voice of the goddess became even louder, more angry. He took more towels down. More lights. More cables. Bags and bags of things. How much stuff could the cave take?

Down inside, the cave was sweaty, salty hot and humid. The entire platform was covered with bulky equipment. The dive equipment was on one side, the camera stuff at the back. Rubbery suits were all around in piles, like empty castes of human worms. It was time for the divers to suit up.

An argument started over on one corner of the platform. The fierce camera lights threw faces into relief. Two divers were standing over the tanks, Alfredo had turned ashen. He sucked his cheeks and looked down at the cables. Horst muscled over to them to find out what the problem was. Ramón became alert to the anger, which had replaced the jocular efficiency in the cave. This was the acid feeling he'd had inside himself all morning. Good. This was good. He had been at odds with the people up till now, but in anger, they had joined him. His index finger found the gun in his pocket and began to tap out a repetitive tune against the side of his leg. Horst called Pedro over.

'Pedro. Come here pliss. Zere iss a problem.'

'Where the fuck is the little runt? I don't believe this.' Ramón was shocked to realise this was Serena's voice. Speaking perfect Spanish. She was looking for him.

Pedro came down the steps, bewildered by the confusion. He walked into a world of bright lights and angry faces and Ramón saw that his father was afraid. He was descending into a devil pit filled with an angry mob that would consume him, tear him apart. Ramón saw his father's body dragged into the crowd, he went down amongst the legs, down and under and what surfaced, what was tossed high into the air in triumph – was gore, his father's stringy limbs tossed high above as the pale strangers gorged themselves, took their revenge.

See, said the goddess. *Do you see?*

Ramón's hand pressed against his gun. He felt its hardness under his fingers and it was out of the pocket and into his palm without a thought. Alfredo and Horst were having a shouting match. Pedro looked shocked – many of the black tubes had been damaged, cut, hacked at by a blunt knife. Pedro looked from face to face as if he hadn't heard. Who would do that?

Ramón was on the steps now, trying to see over their heads, to be at eye height with them all. The gun was in his skinny shaking fingers, the end wobbling like jello. A cartoon gun. He was holding it pushed out from his chest with both hands, cop style. Slowly, the cave filled with silence. Ramón had created this hush, this awe for the goddess. Once there was chaos and shouting and noise and now there was stillness. Hush. Expectancy even.

Yes, yes.

'She doesn't want you here,' shouted Ramón.

With crumpled brows, the faces turn to one another. He had to explain. His father held his hands up, pleading, as if he thought Ramón was going to shoot him.

'No Papá. It's him she doesn't want.' He swung the gun round to Horst. Some people ducked. There was a murmur, a susurrus of voices.

'It's a toy,' said one of the divers. 'It doesn't even look real.'

'It isn't a toy,' stammered Ramón, and somehow in his child's voice this simple truth stood out like rock.

'Ramón.' Pedro tried again. 'It's not your fault. Ijo – give the gun to me.'

Ramón tried not to look at his father. Horst had fixed his grey eyes on Ramón and advanced, winding a path through the bodies, coming on towards the ladder. A moment later Horst was in front of the stairs; Ramón snapped the gun round to face him, holding it close to the colourless eyebrows. Almost touching. Ramón senses were alive; he was conscious of those grey eyes, the pale eyelashes, the sweat rolling down that white chest, the smell of sweat and piss in the cave, the weight of the gun. It felt heavy, heavier than before. His hands shook. Horst was so close Ramón could feel his breath.

'Ramón, no, please!' Ramón looked at his father and Horst swept his arm behind Ramón's knees, forcing them to bend. Ramón's head jerked back and he fell. The gun fired with a hollow *Bam* – just once. The bullet flew at one of the tanks, ricocheted off with a zing, before burrowing into the limestone wall. There was screaming and pushing, both in the cave and outside. Bats flew out and circled the cave. Everybody was shouting.

Ramón banged his face on the side of the ladder, tasted blood and was kicked in the back of the neck as he slipped to the floor. Drowsy, head first, he slid between the adult feet towards the water. The voice of the goddess was clear to him – calm, beautiful, beckoning, calling him; she was down there waiting for him. He was wanted, he was going to her at last. He has done a good thing and she wanted him. He will be with her, hers forever.

Before his face touched the water and his body accepted its coolness, he heard the shouting, the quiet after the gunshot a fading memory. He heard his name. *Ramón! Ramón!* He slipped unnoticed into the water, face first, the natural flip of feet flowing together behind him.

She came to him. She sent her spirits to claim him, and he felt them around him, pressuring him down to her with a press of bodies and faces; he felt their long limbs intertwining and saw their dull eyes and he followed them down to her, gladly, down to where she was waiting, dark, whiskered, enormous, to take him lovingly in her flat wide mouth, and carry him before her into the deep limestone folds, the secret passages of the water filled earth.

Joanna Brown

Love, by harsh evidence,
Thrown from its eminence;
Even God's providence
Seeming estranged

Thomas Hood. 1844

Joanna found the ring by the concrete pier on the north
bank under Waterloo Bridge. She bent to pick up a small
piece of coal and saw the shape of it in the sand. She knew
what it was right away and snatched it up with one hand,
scooping up the coal at the same time. Meaning to have a
good look at it later, not here, where everybody could see,
she shoved the muddy lump into her blouse and continued
her search for pieces of coal with the others. Keep moving,
look for the coal. That was how you earned your daily
bread; she'd watched them and seen what to do. Coal. It fell
into the water when the bargemen carried their baskets
ashore and later, it became lodged in the mud. Gifts from
Old Father Thames to his Mudlarks. Sometimes you got
lucky and found a few copper nails or a piece of iron,
something from the shipbuilders, but that was more round
Whitechapel. You nearly always found coal though and that
was easy to sell. You heard talk of valuable finds, treasure,
coins, jewellery, even whole purses, but those were legends,
myths that kept you feeling with your toes into the stinking
slime, hoping for a better day. Maybe her luck was turning;
maybe she had found something peachy this time. She
patted the damp sandy thing next to her skin, put the piece
of coal into her apron and continued methodically around
the piers. There were fifteen of them scavenging around
Waterloo Bridge that afternoon. She guessed they might
have four hours until the tide changed.

The back of her skirt dragged in the wet, although she had tucked up as much as she dared into the waistband. Her stick tapped the edge of something and she bent to retrieve it. A bone. A cat or a small dog by the look. It went into the apron with the pieces of coal. Her legs were purple from the cold but she continued to feel her way with her toes. She was alert for anything sharp which might pierce a foot and cause injuries; she would starve if she could no longer work the mud.

Her thoughts drifted to the Radcliffe household. The clean beds and plain cooking were a misty dream. Could that have been her life? Was it possible that it was she who had become so desperate, so dirty – feisty, pretty Joanna who had all her life ahead of her? She thought of her bed, with white sheets and a proper wooden bedstead, and everything clean. A nightlight and a book of prayers, which she did not read. That Joanna had been a stupid girl who didn't know when she had it good. This Joanna was paying for it. She bent to lift a piece of rope under the mud, coiled hard and heavy like a ridged eel. It did not fit into her apron so she dropped it into the basket, which she dragged along with her for her finds, although her shoulders ached as if her arms were lead.

The Radcliffe's sunlit house with endless silverware to polish, floors to scrub, steps to sweep. The china dogs on the mantle, clocks she wasn't allowed to touch, the dark portraits that the girls said watched you while you worked. She had hated the work, had complained about her treatment there, but what had she known? She had been warm. And clean. She had a place to go. She had people to talk to. And the young Mr Radcliffe had been kind, hadn't he? He had been charming and friendly and she liked him. She liked the things he said to her, and she liked being noticed. She liked his soft hands and she liked the way he laughed. The others had warned her, but she had taken their words for jealousy and interference. Sarah had taken it upon herself as the senior housemaid to inform her about the previous housemaid, who had been sweet on young Mr Radcliffe. But Joanna had known not to take any notice of Sarah, because everybody knew *she* was sweet on Hepworth, although she thought it a secret.

Joanna shook her muddy basket, and looked through her apron. Only a few pieces of coal today; and not very big. Would it be enough? She needed 2d for a pound of bread and a bit of cheese, and another 2d for a night in the lodging house. She was never going to have enough to buy her way out of this life. She wanted money to buy oranges to sell. A few shillings would set her up. You had to buy your stuff up front. Flowers were the other things, but they came down to money as well. You needed to go to Covent Garden to buy your flowers first, unless somebody fronted them for you. Then they would own you and all your earnings. And most of those girls were a bad lot. There was no money in flowers in the winter, and sometimes not enough money in the summer anyway, so they nearly all did the other. Even the young ones, that was the way of it. But not for her. She felt her stomach. The baby wouldn't move until she lay down to rest. Then it would kick her awake all night. Her belly felt like a cannon ball, a great heavy boulder hanging down between her legs.

No. That was it. Oranges was the thing. When she saved enough, she'd get a stock of oranges to sell and that'd start her off nicely.

There'd been no consequences for young Mister Radcliffe as far as Joanna could tell. He didn't seem aware of any problems in the world, least of all hers. He was always joking and laughing. 'You know what they're like, Joanna,' Sarah had said to her. 'They're all the same, the young men. Madam won't put up with any nonsense again, you know, not after the last one and Hepworth got a right telling off for not keeping better control. You'd better watch yourself.'

*

A wind was getting up, running along the surface of the river, cold and from the North East. The worst kind. Joanna pulled her bonnet tighter to her head. She looked down at her red legs. Would the smell ever wash off, even when she scraped the mud away? The unwanted effluence that London disgorged into the Thames remained in green and bubbling scum on top of the mud, which daily she walked through. She sometimes had a half-waking dream that she picked her way over the back of a poisonous toad, glistening and covered in pustules. She made herself think of oranges, round and bright and sunny, and tried to believe in a future with her child. With a little luck, it might come true, but sometimes, when it was cold, the fear came on her and her whole body shook and would not stop; she feared, no she knew, her end would be here, in the mud. It was hard to see your way out of it. She spied another piece of coal, visible only by a small corner protruding from the slime. It was another small piece of luck. Maybe things could change. She dropped it into her apron and shuffled on through the ooze, never taking her eyes off the wet and glistening surface of the mud.

The water began to seep upwards through the sticky black sand. The tide was coming in; this much was obvious even to Joanna. Lacking experience to judge the tide, she kept a lookout for the others. There were stories of larks trapped by the rushing water, which caught people unaware, cutting off their route to safety. Then you had to swim for it, if you could mind the current. Many of them could swim. She could not. You would have to leave your day's lot if you got caught out. Then there'd be no food and no bed for the night.

She watched the tattered, nameless souls around her. They would not befriend her, they disliked sharing their patch, but at least they had stopped shouting and chasing her off. They had *suffered her to come unto them,* she thought.

She sensed a change in the quality of their searching. They were not so intently scouring the shore, they moved like a small flock of birds, eyes on the sand, bobbing occasionally for a choice morsel, but dipping and wading in the same direction as of one accord. She attached herself to the outer edge of this ragged flock and moved towards the shore with them.

The few coals she had collected were not enough for food and lodging for the night. The piece of rope might fetch 1/2d at the marine store when it was weighed. It must be hoped the ring was worth something. Joanna rinsed it and when she had climbed the Surrey Stairs up from the river, she took it to a doorway where she squatted to inspect it. It was small and narrow, made of gold, and had a death head design on it. The shape was not round, but irregular, with shallow corners on all sides. There was a date and a name on the inside. 15th February 1668. Alex Cheenke. Who was that, this person who someone had loved and wanted to remember? She didn't like the look of it. She wanted to throw it back into the water. It was a piece of luck though, skull or no. Maybe it would buy her the oranges. This could be the start. The problem was, she didn't know who to show it to. The men at the marine shop fenced stolen tools and things the boatmen would buy, but not personal items. The deputies, the men put in charge at the lodging houses, they would fence anything their lodgers would buy, but they wouldn't have lodgers with enough to pay for a gold ring. There were the pawn shops. She could try that, although when they saw her filthy clothing stiff with dirt, they would do her a bad deal. She bit the ring, although she didn't know what gold tasted like. It tasted of the river.

Joanna stood, brushed off her skirts, and rearranged her bonnet. She had lost her hairbrush days ago and had not brushed her hair since. She knew she had lice, picked up from the lodging house and the ragamuffin people she was obliged to share a mattress with. She tried to tuck as much hair as possible into the bonnet and make herself presentable. She also wanted to leave her basket and stick somewhere while she went to the pawn shop and looked for somebody who might mind it for her. If she'd had a coin to give a young boy or girl for an hour, that might have been the trick, otherwise it would be gone as soon as she turned her back. The street was full of people, but none seemed the sort. She set of for Parkers Street, where Jessops was, the only pawn shop she knew. That was where she had gone after she left the Radcliffe's household. She had given up her clothes for enough to buy the rags she now wore and some food and her basket.

Joanna slipped the ring over her thumbnail, made a fist and clutched it tight. This will be the start of something, she said to her belly. We're on our way, baby, right enough. She put the stick into the basket and hoisted it up to her shoulder. Stooping a little, she shuffled into the crowd of people hurrying about their business and made her way along the Strand. Almost immediately, she found herself jostled, was bumped to the side and caught by a lad who saw her steady on her feet with a 'Right ho missus' before he strode off and turned down a side alley she did not know. It took a couple of seconds for Joanna to recover from her flustering. The ring had gone.

The Butler Hepworth, was not so bad looking that a girl couldn't imagine him stealing a kiss. Nor was he so harsh that a girl would shy away from his company. With him, it was only that a girl did not count for very much. To Hepworth, only the Madam was a woman of any consequence. Cook was not above having her say, but she kept to her work and he kept to his and they had less to do with each other than might be imagined. Carstairs had nothing to do with any of them. She took her meals in her room. Hepworth ruled in every other way. Sarah admired him tremendously, that much had been obvious to Joanna from the start. It was said she had once been fond of young Henry Radcliffe but that had changed. Her eyes had followed Hepworth like one of Madam's black-eyed Pugs. She should have looked for a husband, but she remained near at hand for Hepworth.

At first, Joanna could not have given a fig for Hepworth, except to take his daily orders. She knew she had to keep him sure of her willingness to work, so she bobbed and curtsied with the others and it was 'Yes Mr Hepworth' and 'No Mr Hepworth' just the same as the rest. Otherwise she ignored him. And that was fine, whilst Henry Radcliffe paid her his attentions. Soon after she had arrived at the Radcliffe household, the young master had noticed her. She made sure he did. Joanna wiggled and smiled and didn't quite get out of his way fast enough in the hallway, so he had to brush past her and smell the lavender water she splashed on her hair. Sarah tutted and said she was asking for trouble. She was quite ridiculous. Don't think he doesn't know your game. Joanna didn't worry about it. He was handsome and winked at her, and tucked a violet from a nearby vase behind her ear if he got the chance. She certainly preferred his smiling manner to the unmannered boys she had known before. Yes, she had liked Henry Radcliffe thoroughly. And what could she do if he took a shine to her, if he was charming and touched her and held her face and if, before she knew it she had led him on, and even if she hadn't, they'd gone too far and she'd get the trouble of it if she told as well as if she didn't? He had always known that there would be no consequences for him; she saw that later.

The way Cook told it, Mrs Radcliffe had very few favourites, apart from her son Henry, on whom she doted. She favoured Hepworth, her companion Carstairs and her two Pugs, all of whom knew the value of remaining on her good side. Presumably Lord Radcliffe had been in her favour, but since he had preferred Venice to London for many years, nobody of the current household dared an opinion on the matter. After the last girl, Lady Radcliffe had charged Hepworth with making sure 'no such thing happened again', by which he understood that she was not to hear of it again. It never occurred to Hepworth that he could influence the young Mr Radcliffe's behaviour, and in truth, he would not have tried.

It was after she had been in the house for three months that Joanna missed her first monthly. She worried silently, and tried to hide it from the others, washing unsoiled rags out in the sink in the corner of the room she shared with Sarah. Sarah was not fooled.

'Oh for heaven's sake, she hasn't got the sense she was born with,' she said, her small eyes glittering. 'Don't you know we all have our monthlies more or less around the same time? When it was me, yes me, I had the sense to get a cup of blood from the meat larder. Cook didn't catch on for two months, did she? I didn't go and confront Henry with such an embarrassment, no, I went to Mr Hepworth and told him. I didn't want to, he's awful strict as you know, but I knew Cook would start up her clucking and who else was there? Anyway, he was very pleased with me as it turned out, that was quite a surprise. I was a particular favourite of Mr Hepworth's after that; for a while.' Sarah sat on the edge of her bed.

'What happened?' said Joanna, looking at her feet.

'Oh, it's all very well me telling you what to do,' she sighed. 'When I lost it I should have moved on to another house, but Mr Hepworth would've given me a reference. By then I didn't know what to do with myself; when I saw all the, you know, the clots of blood drifting away like that in the bath, I thought I should never go out of doors again. But I was of particular interest to him at the time, he made me feel important, not Mr Henry, skipped off back to

Cambridge and stayed away he did, no, Mr Hepworth made me a kind of assistant to him for a time, well I call it that, and that's when I became the senior maid, not long after.' She looked at her hands which she held together in her lap. 'And if he took advantage of his situation, well it's only natural in a man and there's many a house round here where the butler makes free with the girls. Number 58 for a start, where that Mary works. And number 119 round the corner. I heard that one at church.'

Joanna felt sick and lay back on her bed. Sarah's idiotic ramblings wore her out.

'I don't think Cook likes me, 'Joanna said to change the subject.

'Well, you've got off on the wrong foot. That's all.'

'Did Hepworth like the previous girl, the one they slung out?'

'*Mr* Hepworth, yes he did. She was of particular interest to him, until she left.'

Joanna turned away from Sarah, and tried to hide a sob.

Sarah turned put out the light, dropped her slippers onto the floor and got under the covers.

'You'll get used to it,' she said after a while. 'All his little foibles; his particular interests. You get used to it and you want to please him. I did.'

Maybe, thought Joanna, it was not that Hepworth was an unkind man. It was more that he gave no thought to her comfort, to her feelings or her embarrassment at any time when she had to be in his room. His only thoughts were for his particular interest, his fascination with what she had thought of as her privacy.

The room was well lit, with an overhead lamp and several standing lamps placed around, one either side of the bed and one either side of the large armoire he had for his own use. There were men's hair brushes and what she took to be a cufflink tray covered with a handkerchief on his dressing table, and an old Christmas card that had clearly come from Lady Radcliffe. She remembered the first time she was taken there; the room smelled of his suet hair pomade, and the camphor and myrrh mixture he gargled night and morning. Joanna looked at his bony face, but he did not meet her eye. She felt her legs begin to tremble. He told her to undress and get on the bed. Again, she had tried to look into his eyes, but he removed his shoes and socks and would not meet her gaze. He did not speak to her again. After some moments, she took off her dressing gown and untied the lace at her neck. She pulled the nightdress over her head and lay down quickly, her forearm over her eyes. She hoped he would be on her and quick about it. She was not clean. She had just come from Mr Henry. A little sob escaped her lips, which Hepworth ignored, as he lifted her legs by the ankle, gently bent them at the knee and pulled a large bolster under her backside.

When Joanna had crept back into the room she shared with Sarah, she crossed the floorboards as carefully as she could, tried to climb in without waking her roommate. She thought she was as ashamed as it was possible to be, her heart was trying to get out of her chest and she was cold. She had no words for what had happened to her.

Some nights Hepworth did talk to her. He talked as if he might really be willing to help. He ran his hands over her as if she were a horse, sometimes oiling her skin whilst she stood there in front of the long mirror on his wardrobe and he told her how he was giving thought to where she could go if the pregnancy continued; he said he admired her proportions, she was a feisty little thing wasn't she, standing back to look at her until she began to shake because she knew he was working himself up to something. He liked to come close to her ear and tell her how he was particularly gratified by the engorgement of her breasts, he seemed to relish the word, engorging more each day they are, he touched her and explaining how the swell of them and the darkness of her spreading nipples were very pleasing indeed. Then he would squeeze them, sensitive as they were, watching her face in the mirror, twisting them until she cried out and tried to protect herself. He seemed to like that, he seemed to like her to resist him but if she did he made it worse and if she didn't, he slapped her breasts and made her lie on the bed whilst he sorted through his cuff link tray. Panic rose from her groin to her throat, but it didn't help her.

He placed the mirror on the bed. It was a large oval with a wooden frame. Before long he didn't bother to hide his tray of toys from her any more. He would have her kneel on the bed, her legs spread out properly to either side of the mirror, he said. He would be able to observe all the little things he did to her all the more clearly from now on. Perhaps he would make her look. Do you still think you can fight me, Joanna? We shall have to put a stop to that, shan't we? I think maybe we should keep you here, in a room upstairs where I can look after you properly. For a while at least.

Sometimes Hepworth talked about Sarah. She was as limp a piece of rag as any woman he had known. Once she had ceased to grow, to be a ripening fruit swelling with the Radcliffe seed, she had deflated completely. It was as if he had pierced her like a balloon with one of his tools, but he had not, oh no. He had clamped and twisted, inserted and removed, but he did not often draw blood. On this point he was particular. Now Sarah was as dry and uninteresting as a pod of peas left too long in the sun.

Another time, he was angry with Joanna. 'Do you think Sarah's your friend, young Joanna?' he said, his face so close to hers she could smell the tobacco on his breath. 'Shall I tell you something about Sarah? Sarah will do anything for me; she thinks if she waits long enough for all the strumpet to pass through this house, she'll be married to me in the end. She scurried behind me all morning like a mouse until I finally asked her what it was that had got her so excited. You were helping Cook with the pots because Anny's sick, so she took me up to your room. I expect you know what she showed me. You are a very foolish girl, Joanna Brown. He showed her the box, her little hoard, some stolen coins it was true but most of it given by Henry – the mother of pearl hair slide, a brooch in the shape of an elephant – made of ivory and inlaid with jet eyes, and some money. Enough to live in comfortable lodgings until she had the baby. It had all been in the wooden box under her pillow.

Hepworth made Joanna kneel over the mirror every night for a week. By Sunday, she cried so openly and piteously that he made a decision. He got on the bed behind her, leaned his weight over her back and spoke quietly in her ear. 'The time has come, Joanna. You are to be gone by the morning.'

She tried to turn her head to see him. 'But where will I go, Mr Hepworth?' she said, despite herself. She had known the answer all along.

Hepworth brought her a small bag of things from her room and let her out the back way. He had given her box to Sarah, but he gave Joanna five pounds to start her off if she was careful. He told her to find a clean lodging house and see what work she could do nearby. Taking one last look at the Radcliffe house, Joanna made her way through the streets in the direction of the river. She did not cry and she was not afraid. What could be worse than the particular attentions of Mr Hepworth? As for Henry, he had probably forgotten her already.

Joanna stood in the Strand staring at her empty hand, a small rock in a stream. Motion was all around her, but she was still. It was not so long ago that she was at the Radcliffe's house, she thought, although she had stopped counting the days. She was too tired to count, or reckon with much at all except finding coal to buy some bread and a bed for the night. Now the ring was gone, the gold ring, and she would have to thieve something to pay for a bed. She couldn't think how she would do it. Her legs seemed planted in the street; she might stay here forever, turn into a lamppost and never have to move.

A woman with a wide pannier stopped behind Joanna. 'Scuse me,' she said, and Joanna had to make way. Her feet started up and took her back the way she had come, back towards the river. The tide would be high now, or getting that way and it would soon be dark. From experience she knew the worst lodging houses were better than a night on the streets.

Some lodging houses were bad places but not all of them, although the ones that Joanna might afford now were sinful filthy holes. The one she had stayed in with Hepworth's money been clean and many of the people there were couples, some married, some living like marrieds. There were prayers said for those who wanted them, and a room for sitting and reading. It had cost 4d a night, and that was without food or drink. She would have to find a way to earn some money if she were to stay out of the poorhouse, a place full of the likes of Hepworth, and worse if the stories could be believed. Joanna would sell oranges. She should have bought them the first day she was out, but she hadn't thought to do that and now her money had run out. All she needed was a bit of luck and she would be set up. And when the baby came, well, she'd just have to see about that when it did. Joanna realised she hadn't felt anything from the baby all day. She put down her basket and stick and tucked her arms around her belly. Nothing. Perhaps it was dead. Perhaps it was sleeping. It might be tired, like she was. She closed her eyes. Dead tired. She looked at her basket, stinking with the foul mud of the Thames and, holding her silent belly, she carried on walking down to the water, and left her basket and stick for the quick little hands that would spirit it away.

The second lodging house Joanna had gone to had not been clean. Needing to save her money, she had sought out a cheaper place. She had to share a mattress with another woman, had seen many crawling things in it, on the walls and in her bedfellow's hair. She had not thought to take her bag with her when she relieved herself in the night and it was gone when she returned to the mattress. Shocked at her own foolishness, Joanna had screamed at the woman on the mattress to give her bag back. The woman ignored her, feigning sleep. Joanna had slapped her, after which they had come to blows. A deputy came to see what all the noise was and told Joanna she must leave. It was nearly morning.

She had a bruise on the side of her mouth after that, no money, and no possessions other than what she wore. She had no choice but to throw herself on the mercy of Old Father Thames. The deputy said he was sorry for Joanna, but there was no bag to be found and who could say which one of them had it. She should try her luck with the Mudlarks and pawn her clothes for a basket, try Jessops. It had been a very cold day when she walked reluctantly to the river. It was April but a vicious North East wind carried the threat of snow. That first day, she had stayed close to the banks, her feet cold and sore from the shingle at the edges, the stench of sewer waste and rot catching at her throat. Because the others shouted at her until she stopped following them, she tried to pick her way around the rocks and boulders at the edge. She found the little parcel between a boulder and a piece of driftwood. It was heavy. She squatted to inspect it, which attracted the attention of a woman arriving with a basket of her own. She peered over Joanna's shoulder, her breath smelling of rot and raw onion. Joanna ignored her, unwrapped the brown paper, slipping the string off with difficulty. She put the string on a rock, and the woman snatched it up and hid it in her muddy apron. There was a brick, an ordinary house brick in the second layer of paper. Joanna should have guessed what was in the third layer. She was so tired and dispirited by her night in the lodgings, she must not have had her wits about her. She saw the forehead first. A small baby, translucent white, with almost no hair on its head. Joanna sobbed and laid the baby down in the mud. The woman patted her on the shoulder. 'Poor little mite,' she said. Joanna saw all her teeth were broken and black at the front. 'Still, it's brought you a bit o' luck, all the same.' The woman nodded at the small plank of driftwood that had trapped the bundle among the boulders.

'What shall I do about this?' Said Joanna, pointing at the baby.

'I gen'rally throws 'em back' she said, turning to retrieve a piece of coal she had noticed. 'Best put 'im in the water aways. 'E'll drift orf wiv the current, see.'

It was dark when Joanna reached the shore at Waterloo Bridge. She was hungry. Her baby still hadn't moved. The tide had turned, waves gathering in the centre of the river to pull the water back down to the sea. She picked her way through the barges moored side by side, their keels sucked into the mud. There was no moon yet, but at least the wind had blown itself out for now. Joanna trod onto the stony sand that showed itself at the water's edge. She wanted to go the granite piers, to stand underneath the bridge and look down the water, out towards the horizon. She waded through shallow rushing water, heading for the first pier. The river leaned and turned so often, nobody could see all the way to the sea. You didn't know what was there, just out of sight. If she could walk down the river and just keep walking, she would see something new, be somewhere else, perhaps she would also be different. Fortune might smile on her, if she came to a new place.

An old woman shambled along the waterline, more a heap of ragged clothing than a person. She had a bottle of gin in her hand, which she tipped into her open mouth, then stowed among the many pieces of cloth which covered her. She walked past Joanna, but after a few more steps, turned and spoke to her.

'When's the littl'un due, duck?'

Joanna had no words for anyone. For days amounting to weeks she had wanted somebody to notice her, to speak a kind word. Now she didn't care. She thought only of the freezing water, of the walk down towards the sea, away from the effluence of London, to wherever the river took her. The baby in her belly had not moved for more than a day. If it didn't come out soon, they would both be dead.

'Wanna drop?' said the baggage. Joanna ignored her.

'I had a littl'un drown down 'ere wiv me once.' Her voice was low, a murmur that meandered through her words. 'Right 'ere by the bridge 'e went under.'

Joanna turned and looked at the woman. She seemed to be talking to herself, but then she looked up and smiled, her face so sore and crumpled it looked like red velvet.

'Avva drop, duck. Ere y'are.' She passed the bottle to Joanna, who grabbed it more eagerly than she thought to. She drank deeply, until she felt the burn of it sap the strength in her legs.

'Yep. Me eldest's boy. Arthur, we called 'im. Tryin' to git coal offa barge was'n 'e. Got thrown into the water by the cap'n, an' got caught inna current. Saw 'im go. Nuffink we could do, was there. No.' The old woman took the bottle back from Joanna, replaced the stopper and shuffled on her way, her deep voice rising with the words of a hymn Joanna didn't know.

The river was falling over itself, running and turning itself inside out to get to the sea, swirling at the granite piers of the bridge, trying to pull them with it, pell mell, helter skelter on its way. Joanna headed for the centre. The

134

second pier of the bridge was free of water. She would pass through, under there. She could see the river on the other side, glinting in the weak moonlight beyond. There were gaps in the clouds, and the night was getting clearer, and colder.

Voices. Low, droning, a hard laugh, more muttering. Men's voices. She looked around her, but she couldn't see people. The men might not be nearby. Noises from the opposite bank could sound right next to you. She ran her eyes along the shore on both sides, but could see no group of men. She looked up at the bridge. If that was where the voices were coming from, she couldn't see anybody up there. She carried on, her eyes fixed on the silvery water through the arches. The voices had stopped. Warily, she advanced step by step. The old woman was picking up something from the sand and moving off towards the shore.

The mud had come through Joanna's boots and her feet were heavy boulders sinking deeper with every step. A cold breeze carried the tang of clean salt air to her and the smell of the sewer and grime of London lost its power. Joanna had never been to the sea, and she wanted to go. She could not imagine the sky at the end of the sea. It would be so big and far, who could imagine that? You had to go and see it for yourself. She untied her bonnet and held it to the breeze with one hand, the other cupping her belly. The bonnet had lost its flowers weeks ago and had become a battered ugly thing. She had kept it for the small amount of warmth it afforded her, and for its use as an extra container. The breeze was too weak and did not lift it up so that it fell to her side, heavy in her hand. With a flick of her wrist she cast the bonnet into the water where it caught the current, pulled away from her and disappeared under the bridge.

A rough hand grabbed at her elbow. ''Ere it is' said a voice. 'I got 'er.' Two hulking shapes, like black bears hurried from the darkness under the bridge. Her feet were too deep, too heavy, her legs stiff and lifeless as sodden driftwood. She opened her mouth, but no words came out. Her left arm was pulled with surprising force and she began to topple over. As she looked at the hand on her arm, saw the blackened nails and followed the ragged sleeve to a face like scarred meat, she felt herself wrenched free of the mud. She fell on her side, and smelled the filth of the Thames again. A pain like a stab of lightening passed through her belly. Joanna screamed the pain at the men. The baby had moved. It had only been tired, as she was tired. The grip on her arm loosened for a second, but it quickly regained its hold and she was dragged towards the barges on the shore.

'Git 'er leg.' said a new voice, thick with phlegm. He made a lunge at Joanna's ankle, but she got him across the wrist with her boot. He bent over coughing, wiping his mouth with the back of his hand.

The grip on her arm had not lessened and she was being dragged away from the water. She tried to reach up with her free hand, tried to grab the feet by her head, but she missed and her strength failed her.

"Ere, none o' that!' said a third voice, and kicked her between the shoulders. Her breath left her at once. She blacked out for a second, came round to the smell of death. The first tramp was close, his broken blackened mouth right above her face.

'No,' she said.

A blow caught her across the temple and she gasped. Her eyes slid sideways. One of the tramps was passing a bottle to the other whilst the third had wrapped his hand in the front of her dress, dragging her face up to his. The smell of bad meat and beer was overwhelming. Worse than the smell of sewer that covered them all. He dropped her to the mud, then gripped her throat. Hands were in her skirts, grabbing the layers of fabric, throwing them above her waist. A hand seized her knee and shoved it to the side.

She could hear breathing, fast and hard above her. So this was it. Perhaps she could have become accustomed to Hepworth's interest in her. Tonight, she would be used so hard she would die and be thrown into the river at the end. Father Thames would have her either way.

As she felt the stinking drunken weight of him, she twisted her body to the side, felt one of her legs come free. She swung her foot upwards and managed to deliver a blow on his shoulder that unsteadied him. She twisted her body. She was on her belly, pulling herself by her elbows, crawling away from them. A hand shoved hard on the back of her head, pushed her face into the mud and the stinking filth entered her mouth. She could not breathe. Could not scream. Hands held her ankles. Other hands were on her legs. She was weighed down into the silt by bulk and body. Her belly was crushed into her rib cage and her nose was full of mud. Her fingers clawed, her feet tried to break free of the grip that held them. She could hear nothing but the pounding of her own blood. The child writhed in protest. And then her fingers felt a metal thing. A gift of the Thames. Her right forefinger and thumb pinched around it. She knew what it was. Bless that bastard Hepworth. She knew it was a cufflink. It was caked in sand, but the shape was unmistakable. If it was a good one, with a jewel or in mother of pearl, it would be enough to buy her the oranges. If it was an ordinary plain one, it would buy bread and a couple of nights in a decent lodging house. Joanna forced her head out of the mud, the sudden movement taking the tramp who held her head by surprise. The scream she released from the depth of her belly flew from her body, expelling the mud and excrement from her mouth and nose in an arc of spattering vileness. She bucked to get the man off her. He cracked her across the side of the head with a ringing blow that dropped her face back into the mud, but she drew her clutched fist to her shoulder, her elbow under her chest and lifted her head back up. Two finds in a day. She had lost the ring. She wouldn't lose this.

Joanna heard the whistle. It came again and again. The beaks were here. All the weight lifted from her. She relaxed her body, rolling off her stomach, but did not dare open her eyes. She passed the cufflink across her dress, removing as much mud as she could, and then she put it in her mouth. It was bigger than she thought. She could not do it. It was too filthy. She sat up, not opening her mouth for fear she would cough it into the mud and lose it. The whistle stopped. She could see the old woman with the bottle, making steady progress in her direction.

'Alright, dearie, I'm a coming,' the low murmuring voice drifted towards her.

She heard the slap of feet running on the wet sand. The beaks were giving chase. She didn't look up. Not yet. She swallowed once, twice, a third time, and it went down. It was hope. It was cased in filth, but it was real and shining hope

Day of the Dead

We shuffled through the narrow streets of this half-town trying not to floor anybody with our backpacks and passing handfuls of roasted corn to each other; blue, yellow and red kernels often the size of a fingernail. A small boy waited in a doorway by a drainage channel built by the Incas, or by their slaves anyway. When we were closer to the boy he hissed through his teeth at us, jerking his head to indicate that we should come through the door. He looked about ten years old.

'Yeah, right,' said Shona. 'Go in there and his brother's waiting – with a few friends and a flick-knife.'

'What, even here?' said April. Her mother had texted her every day of our trip, in case she'd been murdered in her sleeping bag.

'Nah.' I said. I had found Peru calming. There are poor people in every country; it doesn't mean they want to kill you. Most people are killed by someone they know, as I could tell you.

The boy was insistent. We ignored him. We ambled through the Incan town, chatting, but the boy didn't give up. He hissed, '*Ssss sss*,' calling us back with a flick of his wrist. He could probably speak Spanish, but he just kept saying the same Quechua words, beckoning to us.

'What's he saying Declan?' said Phil.

'Dunno,' I said. 'Want to go have a look?'

The boy's expression didn't change. He chewed his thumbnail for a moment then turned back the way we'd come, down an Incan street where the houses were behind tall grey walls with only the rooftops visible from outside. When we got to the right place, he nodded towards an opening in the wall, one of the old trapezoidal doorways – a shape that signalled transition to a new dimension; we had read that in a guide book to Cusco. 'Ooh, spooky,' said Shona.

It was the usual arrangement, three squat houses arranged around an open courtyard, the wall by the street forming the fourth side of a square. No electricity that I could see. At head height, washing lines were strung out across the central courtyard draped with colourful fabrics. Ducks and chickens squabbled around our feet, all with their young and all making droppings. A very round woman in a heavily pleated skirt stood in one doorway, watching us. Her face was radiant orange-brown; two long braids hung down her back, joined together at the ends in a U-shape. We had been told before that this prevents your enemy from finding loose hairs to use for bad magic, if that's the kind of enemy you have.

The boy ushered us towards the woman, who we understood was called Mama Qucha. He intended us to go into her house. She wasn't so sure. She planted herself in the doorway; with the granite gaze my Scottish grandmother used, she looked us over one by one. The girls couldn't stop giggling. Shona was picking up her feet, going '*eww*'. April covered her mouth, trying not to laugh. Phil was examining the brickwork, running his finger along the perfect joins. I felt the woman's eyes on me, penetrating, as if she could see me differently. I felt something coming on, like the altitude sickness I'd had earlier on the trip – a hard headache forming into a nut behind my eyes.

Mama Qucha gave way and gestured that we should enter. Her house consisted of a large kitchen with a bed in one corner, a table and two chairs next to it against the far wall. Everything smelled strongly of wood smoke. Two girls came in and sat at the table, shy and pristine in their school uniform with gleaming shoes and white frilly socks and were immediately served a meal of bean stew. Animals were everywhere. We saw several kittens, but no mother cat. There was a small amiable dog and at least fifty guinea pigs, all different colours, fluffy ones and wiry ones, all with crazy sticking up hairdos and mad with timidity. They moved together, running around in squalls calling *peepse-peepse*, but didn't try to leave the kitchen.

The only light came from the open doorway and it took a moment for our eyes to get used to the shadows. The walls were black up into the rafters, ingrained with centuries of smoke and cooking vapours. There were things hanging from the crossbeams, which we realised was food. Whole dried fish as long as my arm, stiff and eyeless. This was the local *trucha* – trout, introduced by foreigners and so rapacious that it was now the only large fish available.

A dusty pair of feathered condor wings was nailed together with the beak and the feet on the left wall above the table where the girls sat quietly eating their stew. On the opposite wall hung three llama foetuses, blind, desiccated and sad, hanging by the scruff of their necks one under the other, their stringy legs dangling down to outsize hoofs. Under the llama foetuses was a blackened trapezoidal recess with a shelf on two empty tin cans. On the shelf were three human skulls, small, with elongated teeth, pushed hard up against a picture of Jesus, haloed and praying, behind a garish bunch of plastic flowers in a tin-can vase.

Shona was taking photos of everything. 'Yikes, did you see this.' I looked at Mama Qucha. She didn't seem to care. Phil was recording. The guinea pigs squealed and fled from his feet. I squatted down and held out my hand for them to sniff but they panicked and swarmed behind a clay pot holding the grass stems that were their food. Phil laughed and continued to record as I advanced on the guinea pigs.

'Grab one and bite its head off.' said April. The squeaking increased as I got nearer, but one tiny nose came forward from the crowd. The other guinea pigs settled down. I felt the children and Mama Qucha watching me. April and Shona stopped laughing as a black guinea pig crawled forward and climbed into my palm where it sat

141

staring with its wonky eyes and mad hair, chewing grass. Mama Qucha sucked her breath between her teeth and cleared the plates from the table. The general chatter of girls and guinea pigs resumed.

I stood up and held the little fellow up to my nose and looked it in the eye. 'Is it a boy or a girl?' said Phil from behind his guinea cam. I was about to say 'How the hell do I know' when a plump hand touched my wrist. Mama Qucha lifted her chin and took the creature from me. She clasped it firmly, which it didn't seem to mind, and held it out towards me, close to my body but not touching. She moved it around me in circles, murmuring softly to it, and then brought it to rest near my face. Boss-eyed, it blinked at me. I began to sweat and wiped my forehead with my sleeve. April had her hand over her mouth and Shona was sniggering, but Mama Qucha was serious. '*Qhate sonqo yuyarina*' she said. Then she put the guinea pig back on the floor with its family. She went back to clearing the table and didn't look at us again. I was nauseous. My headache was getting worse. I felt rooted to the floor, like my feet had pushed through the trampled earth and had taken hold deep under the ancient city where the river, the green Urubamba flowed around me, cool and dark, calming me. All I could see was the skulls in the niche above the fire.

We left the house of Mama Qucha in a daze; I asked to sit for a while in the shade and it was decided that we'd take a break in a small restaurant near the station. It was nearly empty but not very quiet due to the telenovela blaring from the TV behind the bar, and not very cool as no breeze seemed to reach the inside of the buildings there. We'd been there about half an hour when Australian Mike came in.

We had met him a few days earlier, doing river rafting – he taught English to pay for his travels and in Peru, he taught river rafting for an adventure company on the

Urubamba. We had been rubbish at controlling the raft. We couldn't coordinate as a team, we confused which side or what end of the boat was which and although we didn't actually capsize the raft, it was a near thing. It bumped and reared up against rocks we should have avoided, veered into the steep sides of a gully, rolled violently as we skirted a bend, righting itself just in time before the next obstacle as if the river had taken mercy on us at the last moment. Even Mike was freaked when we finally floated up to the camp jetty, or pretended to be.

'I'll tell you guys,' he said. 'That was something.'

We bought him drinks until he liked us. Either that or he forgot who we were. Many beers and Pisco chasers into the evening he got philosophical. The Urubamba is a tough river, he said. He has many faces. In some areas he is fast – dangerous and unpredictable. In other places, he's calm and reflective. He has another name – *Willkamayu* – Sacred River. Sometimes he will reach out to you. When the sun shines, the Urubamba, can show himself to you. You can see right through his body to the rocks and stones. These are his bones.

Mike's words had reached me like a voiced memory, or a dream. I nodded; I was remembering. April had been asleep. Shona and Phil were having one of their relationship conversations. But I knew what Mike was saying here. I got it completely. The Urubamba was benign. Mostly. He could care about you. Be kind. Not like the other river, the black river burnt onto my retinas, always in my mind. The Lot. That bad summer in France, when the dark water was shiny like flowing obsidian, reflecting all the light back at you like a sparkling metal carapace so you couldn't see into the water at all. The Lot does not allow you to know its depths. The Lot will not help you.

Phil was checking his footage from the day, editing on the screen and showing the girls all the gross things on Mama Qucha's walls. The *peepsing* of guinea pigs was audible from the camera so Mike asked us where we had been. We told him.

'Mama Qucha! You're kidding, right?' We looked at him. 'Why?'

'How'd you find her, Declan?' he asked me. 'People come looking for her but they can't get to her.'

'A kid showed us the way. He was her kid, I think.' I thought about it. 'It seemed like a tourist gig. All that stuff on the walls.'

'You filmed this?' Mike grabbed the camera.

He watched it twice. 'She calls herself Alma, but other people call her Mama Qucha. Madre de las Aguas. The old stuff, you know.' We were all listening now. 'They leave votive offerings in the walls, anywhere, because they don't know where she lives – bits of paper with their cell phone numbers on, candles, sweets, stuff like that. They hope she'll give them an appointment, you know. But she never does. And you walk in, just like that.'

'She didn't look like the cell phone type,' I said.

'No wonder condors are endangered,' April emptied her glass.

'It's not actually permitted,' said Mike. 'The foetuses neither. The authorities tend to be a bit more relaxed about the skulls. They dig them up when the relatives have been in the ground for a while. Always done it.' He waved at the bar for another beer. 'She's a shaman. A good one.'

'Oh yeah, right.'

'How's your Quechua Mike?' April asked, squeezing my hand.

'Yeah, what did she say to Declan?' said Shona.

'Play that bit again.'

Another beer got it out of him. 'I reckon it's something like *bitter memories*,' he muttered. 'But I'm not real good at Quechua yet.'

My headache was back. I rubbed my glass across my forehead. The girls stared at me.

'What?' said Mike. 'What's it mean?'

Phil looked at the girls. He patted my shoulder and stood up. 'Alright, Declan? Time to go, mate.' They all knew about the summer in France.

We were fourteen; it was a school trip to this outdoor sports centre where the school went every year, based on the River Lot. They had us out in Kayaks, in pairs. I was in a yellow one, with my best mate, David. We had met at nursery, when we were four and we still played for the same football team on a Sunday – my dad was our coach and his dad was the ref. It was very hot that day, the yellow plastic hot to touch, the sun blaring down on us like a million searchlights. You had to squint to see anything, even with sunglasses.

We worked well together, David and me, we soon got ahead of the others because the river speeds up in certain places, shooting you round the bends. Mr Aldridge, our teacher, shouted for us to wait round the next bend where the water slowed again, and he went back to retrieve a lost paddle for someone. While we were waiting, David and I started goofing around. We stood up, rocked the kayak, sat down quickly. We stood up again, wiggled our bums at the others, who couldn't see us yet. We mooned them. We rocked and wobbled the Kayak, trying to push each other into the water, standing up, ducking down, our arms wind-milling wildly. David reached for his oar and splashed me. I reached for mine. He shook the boat as I leaned forward; I grabbed my oar and using all my weight as a counterbalance, levered myself upright again, my oar slicing round at terrific speed. I dream about his face just as I hit him, right on the jugular.

They knew it was an accident. They said he would have been unconscious when he hit the water. The others paddled round the bend just in time to see David's feet flip upwards and me sit back down in the boat in a hurry. They

145

knew he was overboard and came powering up to us, wondering why I was just sitting there. David was gone. He had disappeared beneath the light and I couldn't see him. I looked. I couldn't see into the water. I looked where I thought the current was going, but he didn't appear anywhere among the metallic sparkles coming off the surface.

Mr Aldridge was alongside in seconds, and I pointed, stammering. He sat still in his Kayak, looking with me down the river. He had a whistle, which he eventually blew, long and loud. He hated himself later, for those seconds of hesitation.

'The life jacket will bring him up again, don't worry Declan' he said to me, but his face was grey and sweaty. Two French sports teachers arrived and he told them what had happened but by then we were losing time. Some rowers who were training nearby, raced away to see if they could find a child in a life jacket. Orange life jacket, someone shouted, as if there might be others.

A radio crackled. A rescue launch arrived, chugging down the centre of the river, people looking each side and dragging hooks through the water. They thought David must be caught on something. A police boat sped past but by then we were all on the bank, me on one side, the others jostling to see. We watched the carp fishermen from further up the river mobilise into groups of twos and threes, their padded canvas jackets giving them a bloated look.

I had a lot of therapy. I *knew* it hadn't been my fault, well – not my intention, but I still dreamed his face. In my dream, I would see his funny smile and his brown eyes looking past me. Then I would see his body, caught in rocks, streaming with the flow of the Lot, long tatters of weed, his clothing and hair drifting in the water. His body would disintegrate into its component parts; his head would come away and bump along the boulders at the bottom of the river until it washed up in front of a recess in the limestone cliff, eddying in a pool by the shore.

The next year, the school nearly didn't go back to the Lot but after that they did. My parents wrote a letter and I went back too, although I wouldn't go on that water again. Mr Aldridge said being allowed back was a way of showing nobody blamed me. I had other reason for going back. I knew I'd find him. It was part of the dream. A hiker had found the life jacket after the spring swell. They didn't find his body, although they said it would turn up eventually. David's parents were distraught. In the dream, I knew I had to search the shore down from the camp; I knew I would find him there and bring him home. Then they would forgive me.

I kept my clothes on and crept out of the tent at night when everything was quiet. There was a wire fence, but somebody had trampled it down behind the toilet block and I could get out without being seen. The Lot was low that year and I was certain David where would be from my dreams, which had been very clear. I would recognize the hollow under the cliff, see some rounded stones clumped together, and that's where he'd be. I did think I was half mad then, but I was certain I'd find him. I stayed in the compound during the day, rubbing my eyes and telling people I had hay fever or a headache; people left me alone.

It took nearly a week of no sleep, but I found him. Not his body. Just a skull. The current hadn't taken it very far – was it his? Who else's would it be? I was sure it was David, although it was smaller than I expected – I could hold it easily in one hand. It smelled of ozone, that green river water smell. I rolled him up in my hoody and got my kit bag from the tent. Then I carried everything over to the toilet block. I had nicked a small Calor gas stove from a teacher's hut and I used this tin bucket they kept under the basins. I boiled David's head for hours; just to be sure there was nothing gooey inside. Working by moonlight, I took

147

out the ball I had brought with me, which was an old-style football with stiff laces. I had already slit several of the hexagonal seams with a Stanley knife, and now I opened the lips and pushed David's skull into the hollow interior. *You're alright Dave,* I said. *You're going home, mate.* I closed the leather again and sealed it with superglue. I passed it from hand to hand – it didn't sound hollow, and it was a strange weight if anybody bothered to pick it up, but it looked like any other battered football. I went back to the tent and lay down. I felt weak, as though I'd been holding my breath for a year.

When I got him home, I left David in the ball. I had a stand on my desk, which used to hold a model of Concorde that we had built together one summer. I put his ball on the stand and there it stayed. But that had not been the plan. The job wasn't finished and although he didn't spook me or anything, I felt I owed him more – he was back, but not home. For a long time, I must have thought I was going to present David's parents with the skull somehow, as retribution. Reparation for killing their son, although they had never said those words to me. They must have thought it though.

I would have to get him out of the ball, maybe polish him up a bit first, before they saw him. Then I would have to find a way to bring the subject up with them. That was going to be tricky because they had moved to Macclesfield, but I could go on the train. Or email them first perhaps. Would they even let me in their house? I didn't think they'd want to sit down to tea and cake with me, and it was the last thing I wanted. Well, I could post it. Yeah – that'd be good. Bereaved parents open parcel with their son's skull in it; read polite note from son's murderer:

Dear Mr and Mrs Sorrensen.
Sorry about what happened to Dave. Thought you'd like to have his head.
Hope all is well.
Declan. XXX

The first thing I did when we got back from Peru was to go online. Everything was finally clear to me and I knew exactly what to do.

David was in his usual place, on the stand. *We're going to sort this, Dave baby,* I told him. I explained to him all about Mama Qucha, this plump little Mother of the Waters with her multi-coloured skirts and her long plaits, guinea pigs and all. I told him about the extraordinary river I had met and how it had reached out to us. It all made sense. David had never really escaped the Lot, and nor had I. We would make our peace with a benign river and be healed. We even had somebody to help us through it. I was pretty sure that was what was going on, but anyway, I would sort it when we got back to the Sacred Valley.

I couldn't wait to get back there. I bought a return ticket to Cusco via Lima, and fifteen kilos of Day of the Dead tourist trash from a Mexican website, because the Peruvians don't go so mad on the merchandising. I was feeling better than I had for years. I planned to get the whole trip done in a long weekend and only call in sick for one day. In Peru *El Día de los Difuntos* – the Day of the Departed is not the whoop-it-up party that it is in Mexico, but I thought it would still be good cover. They do it on November first and second, same as everywhere else. They go to the graveyards and bring all the dead person's favourite things, like music and food and whatever, and they just hang out for hours. If anybody asked me, I would say I hadn't known they didn't go so commercially mad in Peru. I was just a foreigner.

I filled my suitcase with all the Mexican trash – skeleton masks, macabre jewellery, plastic skulls, paper marigolds, two large skeleton dolls called *Catrinas*, a skeleton puppet, a skeleton sombrero, skull torches, a couple of wigs and a skeleton chess set. I also packed David's football, a double cheeseburger just the way he liked it (extra sauce, no pickles), which I had frozen and put in a polystyrene container like they have for organ transportation; also an extendable oar, which he definitely would have liked. With any luck, no baggage x-ray was going to tell the skeleton trash from the real thing in the football.

I made it back to Cusco in the morning of the first of November and caught the first available train to the Incan town where Mama Qucha lived. I took the oar, the burger and the ball out of my bag and left the rest in a locker at the station, which I didn't bother to lock and headed for the bar I knew. It was close to the station. I found it easily and asked the barman if they had any rooms free; he said they had a small one. I paid but didn't look at it. I sat in the corner with a beer and watched European football on the bar TV, trying to think. I had not yet decided how I would find my way back to Mama Qucha's. The bar was empty except for two German girls, lobster pink with peeling shoulders, and a couple of blue-chinned Latinos also watching the football. Then I saw him. Coming out of the gents and still doing up his fly, was Australian Mike. He didn't recognise me until he was on his third free beer.

'Mama Qucha? You have to be invited sort of thing, you know.'

'Look Mike, I think I *was* invited. Anyway, she'll be at the cemetery, right? They all will be tonight.'

A language teacher doesn't earn much and Mike's students didn't have much to give. I offered him enough to keep him in beer and chicas for a while and he said he'd show me the house. After that, he'd be off. 'Don't call me and don't tell anyone you know me,' he said. 'Best if you go back to Cusco tonight. This bar's a shit hole, anyway.'

The house was only two streets away; it looked like all the others. There was nobody around at all, which was good because a six foot white bloke can't hide in an Incan town. The doorway from the street was open. There were curtains over the other door openings, but no proper doors. I couldn't hear anybody. I inched my way across the courtyard, now without any washing to hide behind, and lifted the curtain of Mamma Qucha's kitchen doorway. Nothing happened.

I went in and got straight down to business. There was the smell of wood smoke I remembered from my previous visit. The guinea pigs were huddled in a corner; a slight peep-peepsing rippled through them but otherwise they weren't bothered. I stood on a chair and put the oar up onto the flat part of the rafter where the meat and fish were hanging. That was one of David's favourite things sorted. It was sticky and dusty up there, but he would understand the gesture. Then I got his double-decker-extra-sauce cheeseburger out and put it in the grate under some charcoal remains and covered it with ash. With any luck it would be cremated before anybody knew it was there. Things were going well. I unzipped my sports bag, and looking round the room, took David's ball out and began to cut him free. His skull was as clean and smooth as the day I put it in there.

I reached up to the trapezoidal niche with the skulls and the picture of docile Jesus. I knew there had been three skulls in the niche; everything here was in threes. When I put my hand out, I saw that there were now only two. There was a space between two of the heads. My hand shook; I held my breath and told myself this was the right thing. It was going to be okay, it was as if a gap had been left for him. I put David into the space and got a second shock. He was a lot paler than the other two – they must have been getting the cooking smoke patina for some time, like the walls. Also, his head looked a different shape from the others. My idea of hiding David on that shelf suddenly seemed absurd. Shaking, I held him tight against my chest and stared at the top of his skull.

There was a noise behind me. I turned despite myself and saw a round figure uncover itself from the bed. Impassive, Mama Qucha stood, brushing down the front of her skirts. She shuffled through the guinea pigs towards me.

She held out her hand, neither smiling nor scowling, and took David from me. She wiped her palm over his head several times in a way that was both accepting and gentle, looked into the sockets and then turned the skull upside down. She studied the underside for a few moments, peering into the hollow, and then popped him into her apron pocket, under the overhang of her belly. I felt the prickling of tears behind my eyes and the release of a deep and rigid paralysis I hadn't known was there. She took my hand, stroked my arm and brought me over to the kitchen table where two ceramic beakers of Coca tea had been mashing and were now ready. I couldn't help myself. The relief was enormous and the tears unavoidable. A squall of guinea pigs came to sniff our feet as we sat there together in that ancient room, underneath the condor wings. She bent and scooped up the little black one, which sniffled but didn't make any noise. She put it in my lap, where it looked up at me, mad-eyed and badly coiffed, then settled down and slept. After a while, she spoke to me in Spanish:

'You sleep now. You don't pain. Your friend is safe. Willkamayu know him now. Urubamba keep him now.'

The Tow Path

After Mike Leigh

Yesterday there was a lady sitting on the tree seat by the canal. I was walking Dixie much earlier than usual, so maybe she's always there at that time in the morning but I don't think I've ever seen her before. It's not really my seat, but you get into a habit and I didn't like to ask her to move, so Dixie and I shuffled past the houseboats one more time to see if she had left. She hadn't.

We're all wary round here, because the path has a wire fence boundary with the local primary school and sometimes we get these undesirables hanging around. I don't want to say she looked undesirable. Not at all. She looked a bit sad, and rather tired. Anyway she was there again today. I was early again myself, because I had to start work early, but I was surprised that she was there. She looked as though she might have been meditating or even praying – anyway, she was deep in thought. I didn't want to intrude, so I didn't get to sit down today either. She has short dark hair with quite a lot of grey, cut in what we used to call a pudding basin cut, and she is very thin.

And she was there again this morning. I'll be getting seriously fit at this rate, if I'm never going to get my sit down with the paper again. There would be room – the tree seat is made up of two semi-circles of bench around a copper beech, but you don't like to crowd someone, and anyway, I'm used to having it to myself.

I like these early walks. It's cooler for a start, and I don't know how long this heat wave will go on. The water's turned green and scummy again this year and my hair's gone frizzy. Tony used to call me 'Bog Brush' in the summer.

I don't think she's trouble exactly – I mean she's completely quiet and still – how can she be trouble? It's just that she's there, you know? It's like she's waiting for something to happen and I must say she seems familiar but I can't place her. Anyway, she's not even watching the school. I can't say she looks like she's watching anything much. Just sitting on the tree seat staring at the water.

I saw that woman with the two Dachshunds this morning, also out before it gets too hot; I don't know what her name is but we often stop and talk to each other's dogs:

'How're Ben and Jerry, then?' I asked.

'Much better thanks. Dixie's had a nice trim, hasn't he? What about this heat! You'll be much cooler now, darling!' She often leers her face right close to Dixie and I don't think he likes it very much.

'Ooh yes, he is a handsome devil now,' she said.

'Sweet boy, Jerry. Good boy, young Ben.' I gave them a cheesy treat from my pocket. 'Have you noticed the tree seat recently?'

'You mean that Indian lady? The one that sits on your seat? I sometimes think she's been there all night.'

'She's not Indian is she? She's not wearing a sari or anything.'

'Well I don't know. She could be anything for all I know.' The Dachshunds were not very interested in Dixie, and I decided their owner's not all that bright either.

'What do you mean 'there all night'? She can't have been,' I said. 'They patrol along here you know.'

'Doesn't stop the seats getting graffiti, does it?'

'Well that's yobs for you, not nice Indian ladies' I said.

The Dachshunds waddled off panting, and we went the other way.

It's been a couple of weeks that I've been coming out early and today I sat on the tree seat with my coffee and got my paper out, enjoying the morning sun. That lady was there again but I ignored her, I read my paper although she didn't seem to mind me sitting there and it would be nice to talk to someone from time to time. She seems very pleasant, just sitting quietly. It didn't take long for Dixie to start – he wanted to get up on the seat with me.

'Down Dixie! Naughty boy!'

'I shouldn't worry. I'm sure it's had much worse than that.' She had a low voice for such a small person, with the slight hint of an accent. Probably Indian, I thought.

'It's not a good habit though, is it? We were never allowed to put our feet on the furniture as children.'

'I remember when this seat was put in. 1986,' she said after a pause.

'Do you?' I looked at her, blinking, but she didn't say anything else.

'In loving memory of Samuel Hooper who loved this walk.
1907-1986.'

I remember the flowers left on the seat after the ceremony, multi-coloured chrysanthemums and white roses, soaking wet from the rain. The next morning the flowers were in the canal.

She was there again the next day and I went straight over to her and sat down.

'1986?'

'Mmm?'

'Did you know Samuel Hooper then? Is that why you remember – you know, the seat going in, in 1986?'

'Well yes, I do remember that day.' She smiled at me and smoothed her trousers with the palms of her hands. 'He was my husband's father.'

'I just wonder that I haven't seen you here before. Until recently I mean. I've been coming here every day for more than thirty years. Always had dogs.'

'Yes I know.'

Dixie was pulling to get on with it that morning. Must have had his business to do, but I wasn't happy. I haven't seen her on the tow path every day for thirty years and never noticed, have I?

I left off coming to the path for a bit after that. Dixie had a bit of a funny turn so we just went round the garden of the flats for a couple of days. When we got back to our normal routine, she was there, but walking along the tow path looking up into the trees and touching the leaves with her tiny thin person's hands.

'Morning,' I said as we passed her. We dog walkers do that.

'Good morning, Jan,' she said.

I went straight and sat on the tree seat to wait for her. So, she knew my name. Who was this tiny woman? Eventually, she did come and sit with me.

'1986 was a difficult year for many people you know.' She wasn't talking to me as such. She was facing the swings and just talking.

'How do you know my name?' I still couldn't place her.

'Well,' she said. 'We knew about all three of you in our house, you see. I remember you very well.'

It was when we lived at Brisbane Gardens, number seventy-eight. There didn't used to be that much shouting or anything like that, but you knew when it was happening. If we were doing our homework and trying not to get ink or glue on the kitchen table, there might be a thump on the floor of their bedroom upstairs. David would start his piano practice straight away, and we would all take turns to do our scales and keep going on our pieces one after the other, until we hadn't heard anything for a long time and Dad came down the stairs. He would tread heavily, but

156

slowly, sometimes pausing; he was trying to work out what we were doing before he came down.

'Your mum's got a bit of a headache,' he'd say. Then he'd go out.

We'd nod without looking up and carry on with our homework, or our reading or anything we could find. David would open a can of soup for our supper and we wouldn't see mum till the morning.

After a while, it got so that as soon as the piano started, Dad would come flying down the stairs banging his hands on the wall. I remember the first time; we were all amazed. We just sat where we were – David at the piano and Tony and me at the kitchen table. Dad was white. He didn't say anything at all. He grabbed David by the hair and threw him down the cellar steps. He bolted the door behind him and, shaking a finger at the two of us, he walked backwards up the stairs. The house was quiet till he left that time. We let David out and he warmed the tomato soup for us, purple welts coming out on his legs because he still wore shorts then.

The next time, he threw us all down the stairs. He let us out the next morning before he went to work and we went to school in the same dirty clothes we'd spent the night in. After that, David dragged the old camping mattress from the attic down to the bottom of the cellar steps. We waited by the cellar door when we thought Dad would come. We knew the signs.

When we heard the stamping on the stairs, we went down the steps and stood at the bottom. We looked up into the hall until Dad came to shut the door. It was better that way because you could go to the toilet before you went down there, and you didn't get hurt on the steps. David used to store things down there for us. There were torches and comics, and one of those woven raffia tubes that get stuck on your finger.

*

'Do you have children?' I asked her, although I must have known the answer. I thought I knew why she knew about the three of us now.

'Yes,' she said. 'My son is a pharmacology lecturer in America. California. He's got two boys, fourteen and twelve. My daughter moved to Canada a few years ago with her job. I think she'll stay there.'

'So have you got other family, here I mean?'

'Not really. I have cousins back home; and my younger brother, but nobody round here anymore. My husband died nearly two months ago, and I have been thinking what to do. It was really unexpected you see; I rather thought I would be the one going first.'

I looked at the sky and thought about that for a while. I think my mum would have liked to go suddenly – quicker than she did anyway. She would have been about the same age as Mrs Hooper I expect.

You can't forget these things. Not really. And as a kid, blame is a heavy thing. There was a knock on the front door that night, the last night, and our ridiculous doorbell rang out as well. It was one of those humorous chimes that go on and on. *Bing Bong binga-binga-bong. Bing Bong binga-binga-bong.* The cellar ran under the hall, and you could see up through the gaps in the floorboards – not far, but enough to make out what was going on; you could hear pretty well too. The person at the door had to knock several times.

Dad clattered down the stairs, fury in every step. He ripped the door open and we were all frightened for what he would do. We stared up into the horizontal lines of light either side of the hall carpet and realised dad was moving backwards into the house. A man was at the door. We decided that it must be Mr Hooper from number seventy-six. His voice was serious. We could hear most of it, but it was the tone that impressed us most. Dad was to stop, this was not to happen again, there would be serious consequences and he should know that. He would make sure it did stop. That a neighbour of his should suffer so much.

It went on for quite a while. We all thought Dad would hit this Mr Hooper, who didn't even dare to shout at him. When he had gone, Dad took his keys from his jacket and threw them at the wall. We saw the underside of his feet march towards the door – and then he was gone.

'It was very bad you know.' Mrs Hooper picked at the varnish on the tree seat and didn't look at me.

'What was?' I knew, but I didn't want to say.

'When we came to get you out. I knew something wasn't right the day before, when Edward came back and hadn't seen any of you. I should have come then. I was busy with my own children and the English don't like interference you know. I always wanted to say sorry for that. I should have come before.'

We didn't have anything to drink. We didn't expect to be let out for ages, but it was probably half way through the following morning when we thought something should have happened by now. Normally Mum would have tried to come downstairs or to call to us for school. We hadn't heard anything at all, and David thought we should make a plan of action. Tony and I thought we should stay quiet, but we were getting so thirsty. We heard the post and we knew it was lunchtime. We shouted 'Hey! Hey! Postie! Help! Help! Help!'

He didn't hear us.

The cellar door was impossible to budge. It was scary down there and very smelly by then. We used up the torch batteries looking for things to stand on and any tools. We found a wide chisel in a corner, but nothing else that would help. We rolled up the camping mattress and David stood on it to reach the floorboards above our heads; he could only just reach and he tried and tried to hack a hole between the boards, until he was exhausted. That made a lot of dust and we had to shut our eyes and pant so as not to inhale too deeply. He managed to get the chisel wedged in-between two floor boards and we tried to lift him up so he could push and lever with more strength. It stuck and we couldn't get it to go up or down then. That's what told them where we were – the blade of a chisel sticking up through the floorboards when they came into the hall.

'I remember your face, at the top of the stairs. You were like an angel, with the light from the kitchen shining behind you.' She had been quite chubby then, with a long plait down to her waist.

Mrs Hooper looked up into the leaves above us. I was fiddling with Dixie's lead.

'In Sri Lanka, someone would have come the same day your father left. We didn't realise how far gone your mother was, you know. I always thought it would have been different if I'd followed my instincts. It was years before I could hear an ambulance without thinking it would be too late.'

'We've all got things we wish we'd done differently,' I said. 'David always thought he should have done something for mum. Did you know he died in the Gulf?'

'My son told me. He always knew about you.'

I remember Mrs Hooper's children, quiet and wide-eyed when we were taken next door that day. And I remember the food. Mrs Hooper's cooking. It was the best food we'd ever tasted. The kind of food that lets you know you're alive and that you're eating somebody's love into your body. The smell of those spices always meant comfort and safety to us after that. Whenever we moved to a different foster family, we asked if they could cook Indian like Mrs Hooper, but they were rubbish at it. We used to get every type of curry whenever we could, but especially with fried dhal balls, samosas, meat roti and that coconut pickle – coconut sambol. Whenever we got back together again, we'd go out for a curry.

Maybe you don't know what a beacon it was, I thought.

I had to go to Leeds for a training course and I left Dixie with my neighbour for a few days. When I got back, the weather had turned. It rained, which made bubbles on the canal water and the wind blew leaves down onto the path. I wondered if an Asian lady who lived in this climate for long enough would eventually get obsessed by the weather. Why would she stay here if she didn't have to? Anyway, she wasn't around for a few days.

When I did see her again, she was sitting on a plastic bag on the tree seat, reading a book. I didn't like to disturb her, so I walked round with Dixie. I knew we would have to finish our conversation, but I didn't want to. And then again, I did want to.

'Hello, Jan.'

Her quiet voice was at my back as I walked past and I stopped without turning round. I thought – if I sit down next to her, I don't know what might happen. I could just nod and move on, carry on up past the Emily Rose who was back on her moorings, and just keep going. In the end, my feet made the decision for me – they wouldn't walk any further; I was wheezing and needed my puffer. Mrs Hooper took up almost no room on the seat.

It was very hard to get the words into my mouth. I hadn't talked about it for so long. Not since the trouble with Tony came to an end and I think that was nearly fifteen years ago. I don't count these things exactly. I always know everybody's birthdays, but the deaths, the bad things, they get a bit fuzzy; although I know the time, to the minute of the day when the anniversary comes round. I hadn't thought there was anybody left who knew about it all.

I tried to slow my breathing. 'You did save our lives, you know,' I told her. 'We didn't know how to be grateful enough.'

'I know, but your mother… If I'd been quicker, it could have made the difference.'

'Maybe.'

I pushed myself right back into the tree seat and leaned against it, my legs swinging freely underneath. Nothing good had ever happened to my mum.

'Mum just couldn't hold onto any hope. Years of being told you're rubbish, being treated like rubbish and being kicked around like rubbish don't let you hope for much.' I said. 'I think she just let go.'

She patted my hand and stared at the water. 'Tell me what happened to Tony. We did see him occasionally, not in a very good state, you know.'

I had known it would be Tony that she would ask about. I wanted her to ask about me. I'm the one that's still here. I'm the one that's managed to hold on; but she had a soft spot for Tony. Little Tony. She's tough, is Jan. Jan'll be alright. Jan's brave. It's the boys I'm worried about.

'Poor Tony,' I said, after a while.

By the time Tony was twenty-two, his brain was rotten from the inside out. He had been through a few institutions by then, but nothing helped him. He was very clever they said. It made him difficult to treat. He always thought he could out-think them, which might've been true; more's the pity for him.

He was a secretive boy and didn't talk much. I knew him pretty well, though. From the time we went to our first foster family, the Johnsons, I knew he was working on how he was going to find Dad, until he thought of a way to get him back for what he had done to Mum. He got so angry, so frustrated with himself, that he would implode with drink and whatever he could scrape into a roll-up. He was fifteen when they first said he was an alcoholic.

Tony had maps and plans and kept notes in a book, which he never let anyone see. He liked computers and the school encouraged him. Then he tried to hack police records looking for Dad and he was taken away from the Johnsons', but he was used to the back of a police car by then. When I next saw him, on our own, he didn't want to talk to me – not about his plans and his secrets, only to ask about David. He was still obsessed though; find Dad, pay him back – that was all he could think about. He told me he was going to live on the streets because he reckoned Dad must be hiding there; he hadn't found any records of Dad being employed, being sick or having died, so what else could he do?

I always thought Dad would be on the Costa with all those other nasty bastards, but Tony didn't think so. 'Too much of a loner,' he said. I never asked what he'd do when he tracked Dad down, but I reckon it would have been fine by me. David – he worried in a soldier's way that whatever Tony did would only damage him more than it hurt Dad; he told him it was best left.

Tony did live on the streets. He walked a long way sometimes. Occasionally he would come to me for a bath, and said it was like he was making a documentary, undercover, but not mad with it or anything. That was short-lived. After about a year, I didn't hear from him unless the police or social services contacted me. They were usually pretty good with him, but I tried to be as quick as possible getting to him. He liked to be out of doors, did Tony.

Then there was this particular summer that I thought I could afford to go away for my holidays. I'd never been away from round here. Eventually I got a few pounds together, but had I always thought I shouldn't go anywhere

163

in case Tony turned up, or in case he found Dad. I went for a week although I knew it was wrong.

This girl from work, Linda, she had relatives up that way who owned a caravan near Rhyl. It was lovely. She liked the boys, did Linda. I was her ugly friend that made her look good, but I didn't mind. I met all these people and I had a nice time. The beaches were beautiful.

Anyway, when we came back, there was a note through my door to call the police. I knew what it was the moment I saw it. David was away on training somewhere, I forget where, and I just turned straight round and went to the police station. Left my bag there in the hall; it was still waiting there when I got back.

'Tony – he, Tony got run over, Mrs Hooper.' It was hard to say the words. 'It was a hit and run driver.'

She looked at the green water and didn't say anything.

'I always thought it was him – you know, my dad, but nobody ever proved anything.'

'Oh Jan.' Mrs Hooper's voice was croaky.

I knew then she *had* noticed me and knew what I'd been through. Somebody knew about me – I was *real*. I existed.

And that was it. I couldn't do it anymore. I could hold on all that time, through all their deaths and all the empty years afterwards, but as soon as she said that, I was over. It was the end of me. I cried and cried and cried. A little boy with a football came and looked into my face – puffy pink ugly head with tears streaming down it, but I couldn't stop.

Mrs Hooper held my hand as we sat on the tree seat together. I realised that apart from Dixie, I hadn't physically touched another person for a long time. After a while, Mrs Hooper went and bought us both a flake '99 from the van outside the school. I looked at the canal and the boats until she came back but when she gave me that ice cream, I cried again because I'd finally recognised the one person left in the world who knew me.

Sand Tranny

I: Stephanie

If the tide was out enough, I'd usually see Toby down on the beach on my way to work. I'd go up on the Millennium Bridge and then I'd look back at what he was doing, before heading across the water. Sometimes I saw him there twice a day, even in the cold. He was famous for a while. Or *they* were. The Sculptor and the Sand Tranny. It's on YouTube.

Toby worked his bit of sand on the beach in front of the Tate Modern, which is where I leave Elvis in the mornings. He says 'Ciao Bella' and off he goes. We met at college in Manchester, back when we were doing the Museum Studies course; we've both ended up in London.

Once I'm over the river, it's past St Paul's and more or less straight up to the Museum. That's the Museum of London, not the British (I wish), which would be Waterloo Bridge. I could get there just as easily, but then the walk wouldn't be along Southbank, which I love in the morning.

Toby I knew from before-before, through my sister, he'd been a friend from her art student days. I used to whistle as I passed and he'd wave back if he heard. Sometimes he was too engrossed, digging out or smoothing off with a water spray. I couldn't do it, letting everything I made get washed away – I'd have to take a picture of every sculpture I ever made if that was me.

The subject of the sculpture was always the same with Toby. A sofa. He would make a sofa out of sand and then decide who was going on it that day. Sometimes it was a Suit, a politician. Sometimes a Mullah. Sometimes a thing, depending what was on his mind. A vampire, a daisy, a horse's head. Boris. An enormous pear. The Queen – that got him a lot of tips. Mrs Thatcher once, when she died, handbag and all. He put one of those Halloween props over her head – a bloody knife on an Alice band that was supposed to look like she'd been stabbed ear to ear.

When Sal, my sister, had been at art school with Toby we'd had a few drinks off and on, as a group. He was fun. He was a drinker though, even then. I don't know which of them stuck college out the longest. When she went on her travels I didn't see him for years, until there he was – making a sofa out of wet sand by the Millennium Bridge.

It was around late May that Elvis and I began to notice the sculptures were different. They became less topical. Soon it was two people on the sofa more often than not – a man and an enormous woman, very tall, well-endowed, great legs. Too fabulous, obviously, but it still took me days to realise it was a man in drag sitting next to Toby.

'G honey – Your friend's in lurv,' said Elvis.

'Looks like,' I said.

Soon baubles and bits of decoration started to appear on the woman, whilst the man seemed to get smaller, making room for her bling. Sometimes she had a tiara, sometimes a wacky blonde Miss Piggy hair-do, sometimes both. That got Elvis's attention. He could do hair as well but it was wigs where he was the expert. Elvis did Egyptology at uni first time round and to most people the wigs in all the wall friezes, those Cleopatra haircuts, they all look identical, but they're not. If you know what you're talking about, you can date a piece of Egyptian art to a certain time period by the hairdo. When he realised that's more or less the same for most periods in history, he got interested in working for museums. So Elvis did Museum Studies next, which is where we met, and a wig-making course to see how it was done. His flat is full of wigs – there's a Victorian orientalist one on a plastic head in the guest toilet and if you stay the night, the bedside tables have Pompadour headgear on them which take up so much room so you can't put your tea cup down.

Sand Tranny had a varied wardrobe, but the hair was always the same. Long, blonde and glamorous, like a showgirl. Sometimes she might be wearing a glossy belt cinched around her middle, massive dangly earrings or the boa, which was a favourite. Then the shoes arrived. Sand Tranny had a thing for shoes.

'Goes with the T-Gurl turf,' said Elvis as we hung over the railing one day at lunch.

It was cold and Toby was got up like a World War I pilot, a handlebar 'tache glued onto his upper lip, leather sheepskin jacket and yellow scarf sticking out on a coat hanger. He hadn't noticed us. Elvis waved his egg and cress Sub towards the shingle and spoke with his mouth full. 'Shoes is what it's about with your average tranny.'

'Really?' I said. 'Here's me thinking it's the make-up and the prosthetic bosoms, implants and stuff.'

'Na – shoes. Take it from me.'

Mostly Sand Tranny's shoes were red. They were all impractically high. Her favourites were a pair of sequined raspberry stiletto stacks, very Priscilla. God knows where Toby got them. I'd seen smaller mobile homes.

I only met the real thing by chance the first time. She was stunning. I was crossing over the bridge to nip into the Tate, the Lichtenstein exhibition was closing and I wanted to see it. I nearly walked past them. She was standing on the bridge with Toby in a navy blue pencil skirt with a close-fitting top in Breton stripe, and a black patent shoulder bag dangling towards the water. Her arm was round his waist and they were both looking at the sand sculpture. I tapped Toby lightly on the back and he swung round and planted a couple of kisses on my cheeks. I got a kiss from Stephanie too. She smelled of Marc Jacobs, which I liked but couldn't afford.

'Hello love,' she said. She had a dimple near her mouth but only on one side.

We looked at the sand figures. Stephanie nodded with an appreciative *mou*. It was like a sepia 3D photo of them at home, with the colours touched up like my granny's wedding photo. He was sitting with his ankle across his knee, which I knew is a tricky thing in sand because one knee is unsupported. He had his arm round her shoulder. The sofa blended in with the riverbank wall, grey-black and damp. The Toby figure had a baseball cap on, the wrong way round; the Stephanie lookalike was tall but demure, looking over to the North bank with both hands on her own knees. Toby said her wig was secured with a stake right down between her shoulders to stop it flying off.

The real Stephanie's hair was straight and flat, not coiffed and curly like the wig. It was long and blonde, and in great condition. I tried not to stare, but I had to know; I checked out her hairline as best I could but if the real Stephanie had a wig on, I couldn't see it. Not even braids – it was her own if you ask me. Long and blonde and to die for. Only the shoes were wrong. The real Stephanie had black ballet pumps on, probably to keep her height down. I kissed them and left with promises to 'do drinks very soon, Dahlinks,' and nipped into the Tate. They were holding hands when I looked back, and Toby was pointing at the water.

We met up with him about a month later.

'Here we are,' he said, putting three pints down.

We were at the Founder's Arms on Bankside, a bit grey unembellished concrete as pubs go, but handy for meeting after work. I huddled in my cardigan; they'd put the heaters on so people could sit outside and watch the river but it wasn't what I call warm. Stephanie was on her way, which could mean she'd be there in a minute, or in an hour according to Toby. The tide was up, so he hadn't been down to the sand. He looked very clean. Crisp, like a shiny red apple.

'I was very sorry to hear about Sally,' he said. I nodded into my glass. Elvis sucked his breath and watched a police launch going past.

'Yes,' I said.

We sat in silence for a while. The pub was full of tourists, probably going to the Globe a couple of hundred yards away, along the path.

'I've never actually been,' Toby said, meaning the theatre. 'Have you?'

I nodded. I was going to cry if I didn't get my act together. Christ. Talk woman.

'I've seen a couple of things,' I said in the end. 'One was filth.'

'What, a Shakespeare?'

'Na. More like a modern wannabe – they had people dressed up as Roman gods and shagging all over the place.'

'Well fuck me,' said Toby.

'We'll see,' said a light voice behind him. Stephanie pulled up a chair next to Elvis and crossed her legs in a motion that made me think she'd practised in front of a mirror. She inserted a Marlboro Light into a holder and lit it with a gold lighter; it felt like the whole of Bankside stopped to watch her. Toby was cock-a-hoop. He ran to the bar to get her a white wine spritzer.

I was drinking beer, and I didn't smoke anymore. If I could have had one or two and left it there I wouldn't have minded, but I knew I was like an alcoholic with it. Just one and I'd buy ten the next morning and twenty the day after that. I would spend my whole day at work thinking when I was going to get my next cigarette. Best not go there. I carried on talking about the Globe as if it had been Stephanie who had asked the question, trying to breathe in her smoke.

'And this other time, I saw *King Lear* I think it was, and we had seats for that one. There were a bunch of Americans in the row behind, or maybe Canadians, and they knew the play back to front. They were waiting for every joke and punch line and laughed their heads off. They were having the best time. I don't think anybody else knew the play as well as they did.'

'I hope you gave them a mouthful?' said Elvis.

'I thought about it, but when I turned round – I was going to start with a stare, you know and work up to the *tutting* – they all had deerstalkers on. About ten of them all. They must've been over to Baker Street. You had to laugh. '

'Thanks pet,' said Stephanie as she took her glass from Toby and patted the seat next to her for him to sit.

'What d'you do fer a living, love?' she asked Elvis.

'I'm at the Tate – Modern, for the moment yeh. I do the memberships.'

'Oh,' she said. 'That's nice.' She squeezed Toby's hand and sipped her spritzer.

Elvis asked him how they'd met.

'What, me and Stephanie?'

'Yeh.'

'Gorgeous, isn't she?'

'Yep. Gorgeous.'

'She's seen you before.'

'Eh? I would have remembered.'

'Yeah, she's a guide at the gallery – the Modern...'

Elvis nearly choked.

'What – I've never.'

'Lawks,' I said.

'Yeah – she's Stephen at work. Well, we'd got chatting and that when I went in for a tea once, and he, she said, only it was he that day, he said he could probably get tickets to the Hockney at the RA, did I want to come?'

'Ooh, *ni-ice.*'

'Gold dust.'

'Yeah, well I turn up and wait in the hallowed porticos and after a bit, when I thought nobody was coming, this woman came over and asked if I'd like some tickets. It was her. Quite shy and that, and I was so stunned I just followed. The rest as they say, is history.' He was fit to burst.

'Yeh, we had a ball.'

'Boom boom' I said.

'How are Sally's kids?' said Toby narrowing his eyebrows.

'As you'd expect.' I looked at the water. 'Peter's still at school. Living with John's mother, poor lamb. Even she thinks John's too much of a wanker to be trusted with his own son. Zoe's alright, I think. She's gone to South America, with some friends.'

'Ah, gap yah is it?'

'I think you have to have been at school for longer than five minutes for it to be a gap yah. She's skipped off with some cash her daddy gave her, and we haven't heard a word.'

'Has he heard from her?'

'Not that I know of.' I emptied my glass. 'I'm not exactly talking to him.'

'Gina – I was *so* sorry about Sally,' he said again.

'Yeah, alright, I'm getting that.' I said.

'Oops,' said Stephanie. 'Look pet, I'm going to get off now.'

'No – don't go,' I said.

'She's got to get ready,' said Toby. 'The WayOut Club. She's doing an escorted night out for some virgin inbetweenies. '

'Yeah. Anyway, I'll see you later. You catch up. Tarrah.'

'You not going?' I asked Toby.

'Nah. Not in the mood.'

Stephanie slipped into the crowd walking along Bankside, weaving her narrow hips between the tables. Her blonde head rose above the stream of dun coloured hair by at least six inches. The entire pub watched her go.

A while later the tide had gone down some. I was sitting on the damp steps getting a cold bum and lighting one of the fags Stephanie had been good enough to leave on the table. Toby was showing Elvis how he made his sofas, only they didn't have any tools so they were using their shoes. The inside to dig with, the sole to smooth with. I lifted one of the bottles we still had left, concentrating on not getting any drips down my front.

'Nah, nah – srong. You… afta… do-it like this.' Toby demonstrated how to smooth the surface of the sand with a trainer, for the third time. Elvis was never going to get it. He came and sat on the steps with me. I applauded.

''Sready.' Toby said, and we heaved ourselves over to the sofa. It was wet and a tight fit for three but it held. We sat and looked at St Paul's.

''Samazin', innit?' Elvis put his head on my shoulder but I pushed it off. He smelled of sick.

Toby and I finished the bottle I had and he got up to bring another one from the steps. Elvis snored.

'No, no, see, I really was *sorry* about Sally. It was horrible. Horrible.' Toby said. I knew we had to have this conversation. It took me a while, but in the end I got the words out.

'Nobody knows why she did it. OK.'

'O-*kay*.'

'The end.'

'Yep.'

'Nobody…knows.'

That's what everyone wanted to know. They'd all heard the how, but nobody knew the why. Not even John The Bastard, her wanker of an ex. He reckoned her life had been pretty fantastic. It had definitely improved after he left. I wouldn't have called my sister easy-going, or said she didn't have a care in the world. She had plenty of shit in her life and she could be a handful, she'd been unhappy, drying out again – it was tough, I knew that. It was more that she just hadn't seemed the type. I'd have thought she'd keep it hanging together, for the kids no matter what. And, although I didn't admit this to anybody and I didn't like myself for it, I hadn't thought she was brave enough. Or desperate enough.

Toby said he'd seen her around on and off but she hadn't spoken to him about anything much. 'Just a chat. How you doing? Sort of thing. No big. You know?'

'Well, *big* was fucking happening and we didn't fucking know about it,' I said. 'Somebody knew. Christ. '

We held hands and watched the tide come towards the sofa.

'You'd better get off home, Toby. Stephanie'll hate me if you don't get back before her,' I said.

''S'alright, pet, she already does.'

'Great.'

We woke Elvis and nudged him up the stairs. The sofa was gone when I walked past next morning. The waves were right up to the steps.

Sal and I did a lot of Ouija when we were younger. We pushed copper coins or dad's shot glasses around and scared ourselves silly. We never owned a real board, bought from a witches' shop or anything. We made our own boards. We even sold some to our friends, especially some girls in my year at school. We'd spend a whole Sunday designing the letters alone and each board we made had its own style. One was medieval, and looked like the letters were carved from blocks of stone. Sal put gargoyles in the corners, which gave me nightmares later. There were different themes, horses, dolphins, vampires, but she usually put one of us in as the beautiful sorceress figure in the centre of the board. She was the real arty one and I was her assistant, allowed to fill colours and follow her plan. My

173

absolute favourite was the dolphin one where she was a mermaid princess with three dolphins circling round her; we kept that one, although I don't know where it is now. She made a sorcerer's Ouija board for me once, with dragons curled round the edges. I watched the perfect drawings unfold from her mind in total admiration. She put me in the middle dressed in long white robes with dramatic makeup and a crystal ball in my hand. We never owned a crystal ball.

It has occurred to me more than once since she died, to ask her what happened. I lie in bed and I can't get it out of my head. Why did she do it? Was it really on a whim, like John The Bastard says? She was an instinctive person, but taking your own life – I can't see it.

I feel Sal close to me when I lie in bed, like I can smell her skin. I still have the sorcery Ouija board. It's in the dresser. Not in this flat. In the other one, Bunyan Court, the concrete matchbox our dad left to us, when he died. I don't go there much these days. I've got a lot of good memories about Sal though because we lived there together for a while, but John, her bastard of an ex uses it now, defiling her bed with any stupid woman he comes across and paying a cleaner to go in twice a week after him. It's complicated. I'm supposed to rent it out, but I haven't got round to that yet.

She's in my head, at night. If I meditate, clear my mind, which I'm not good at – a lot of stuff seems important and I want to write it down so I don't forget, but you have to push all that away, keep returning to a word or a thing, a focus that sends the crap away. My word is Sal. If I say her name, and let everything else go, she talks to me.

She says it's fine, where she is.

I try asking, what's it like?

She says oh, like being on a beach holiday, you don't think about it much, you just relax.

I'm not sure she knows she's dead. I don't like to ask. It's ridiculous. Probably I'm stupid, but I worry she might, perhaps, get a shock and stay too long in limbo if I tell her something and she realises all of a sudden what's going on.

I say I miss her.

She knows. She misses me too.

She has visited with mum, which is good because they didn't speak when mum was alive. Eventually this will occur to her.

She asks me about Zoe. She says she hasn't heard from Zoe.

I don't know if that's a good thing or not, I tell her – nor have I.

I have asked JTB, but he's not worried. No news is good news. She's in Brazil, having the time of her life. Due to go to Cuba at the end of the month.

Sal says Cuba's not as much fun as you'd think.

She knows her son Peter is alright. But can I look for Zoe for her?

I say, I can.

And I can. I can use the Tarot.

I have several different packs of Tarot. I even have one from Cuba, funnily enough. El Tarot de Cuba, an antique pack, the cards are old and creased; the pictures are all of tiny birds and white children in tropical paradise, by the satin soft Rio Miel – the Honey River which is round the coast from Guantánamo. I don't use those ones. They're not lucky for me.

When the cards are sweaty, like money, they carry the smell of somebody else's use, and they don't speak to me properly; they do their own thing, not related to my questions. It takes experience to notice that. Some people like to use old cards but I have to have my own to work with. They have to be new and fall from each other in an easy cascade. Then they are free to tell me the truth.

175

I have looked for Zoe. I will have to find the right time to tell Sal what I think. I will have to go and see John The Bastard first.

I don't think Zoe will be going to Cuba, I say to Sal. I don't think she's going anywhere for now. It's not danger. It's too late for that. Zoe is in stasis. It's the four of cups on every deck I try. Sometimes the Hanged Man as well.

She must be sick, I have decided. In hospital I think. It might be a coma, because of the stasis. I would have thought Sal could feel that, as if Zoe is half way to where Sal is, hovering, but I don't know how to ask that either without Sal throwing a wobbly. I will get hold of that bastard John and make him check Zoe's credit cards. I want to know how long it's been since she spent any money.

It took about two weeks for me to see the change in Toby's sculptures. Normally he smooths the skin with a water spray and a flat trowel. He can give it an impression of polished granite that almost gleams. The sculptures looked unfinished half the time now. Once or twice, he was on the sofa alone. No Stephanie.

'Ay-up,' said Elvis.

'Indeed,' I said.

More noticeable than that, was the mad bling that appeared on Stephanie's avatar, when he eventually put her back on the sofa. The Miss Piggy wig became insultingly dishevelled sometimes cocked over one eye. Her beatific smile was replaced by a deep 'o', her hands stuck out in front of her, palms facing; and she didn't always have her boa. The raspberry spangled stilettos were always there though, now sometimes half on – half off, as if she'd turned her ankle in them.

Elvis said Stephen was evasive at work, tired and touchy. I tried to talk to Toby, but he wouldn't stop and chat, he had no time for drinks with me, although I could see he was half out of it most of the time. We were busy at the

Museum and I didn't have a chance to chase him up. I wish I had. At the end of the summer term, we always get school parties at the museum and for a few weeks in June and July, the place is packed. We have to prepare the new exhibits, check that the annotations are up to date and write our talks for the school groups, all at the same time as our normal work. You wouldn't believe the amount of stuff that comes in every week. It all has to be catalogued and packed away, not necessarily in that order. All the stuff people have dug up or found in granny's attic. We have a weekly meeting with the Mudlarks to see what they've found washed up by the Thames, but I don't do that unless they want to show me a coin or something. I'm on the Roman London team.

Elvis was getting to know Stephen at work a bit better by then. He said he was a nice guy, easy to talk to and very knowledgeable. He'd been in the Damien Hirst coterie for a while, but not that close because he hadn't gone to Goldsmith's. They met up for lunch most days and if I hadn't been so busy, I might have felt left out. Elvis said they didn't talk about relationships, they talked about art. So he had no idea what was coming either.

I got a text from Elvis. It was a Monday, early in August.

u'd betta cum.

I was working on my 'Roman Matron in Londinium' blog. My baby. The aircon had fused its circuit again, sweat was running down my back and the frilly blouse I had to wear stuck to my skin, the long skirts and petticoat got in the way and the boots were too small. I'd been told to volunteer for the Dickensian Experience tour. I was a street vendor they said and gave me a bunch of lavender to prove it.

wot, I replied.

trble

wot trble

177

for fuks sake get yr ars down here.
Kk

u cumin?
omw!

I left the Dickensian costume on the back of my chair, remembering the bonnet at the last minute. Dithering for a moment on London Wall, I decided a taxi would take longer than walking and fretted all the way to St Paul's. I ran over the bridge, grateful not to be wearing those heavy skirts. Elvis was waiting. He looked fine, no sign of injury. I bent over, panting, feeling tricked.

'What you playing at? I haven't got time for…'

He pointed over the railing at the sand sofa and did a sort of sideways jerk of his head that said 'I told you so'.

'Oh fuck!' I said. 'What does it mean?'

'You tell me. He's *your* friend.' Elvis crossed his arms.

'Hey – don't put this on me! Where's Stephanie?'

'Not at work.' He turned his back on me and stalked down the bridge to the chimneyed monolith that was his workplace.

It shocked me. Sand tranny was half off the sofa, half on, head back, her wig and boa in disarray. But the horrible thing was the shoe. There was only one of them, and it was in her eye. The spiky heel of one shoe had been jammed right into her eye, the raspberry spangles glinting like bloody fish scales in the salt breeze.

I rang Toby's number. *Shitshitshit* – answer Toby! It went to voicemail. I texted him, my thumb suddenly stiff. No reply. He didn't always reply anyway. I decided to go down to the sand. People had gathered on the railings, gawping and pointing, there was nervous laughter from a group of Japanese teenagers. Some people were taking photos. A man in a suit was playing a piano that was chained to the railings – part of some arts initiative that summer; it was a soft and lilting piece so inappropriate to my feelings that I thought for a moment, it'll all be fine, this is someone else's dream.

The tide was coming back in and with it the wind, which pulled at my blouse. It was getting cold for the end of summer. Toby wasn't there. He'd left his tools behind, thrown against the wall by the looks, I thought he would be around somewhere. I didn't know if this meant he'd done that to Stephanie, or that he wanted to. I called again. Still nothing. I decided to walk along the beach but I knew you had to keep an eye out for the tide. You can get cut off if you don't know what you're doing. I didn't have a clue.

I could see there wasn't anybody on the Blackfriar's side, so I went the other way, towards the Globe. The river turns a corner after Bankside pier as it goes under Southwark Bridge, so you can't see back to the Tate and the beginning of the Millennium Bridge from there. Bloody Elvis. He could have helped. Just as I started to run I saw Toby, huddled against the wall, his knees drawn up, his hands over his mouth. Beer cans lay all around him and he'd pissed his trousers. You couldn't see him from the Bankside path, but if you could have, you'd have thought he was begging, although it would have been a stupid place to do it.

I got him to stand up, he was shivering and as I helped him zip his jacket up, I saw the blood all over his shirt. His eyes looked past me and tears flooded down his cheeks. I told him we were going to the police and he just nodded. I put my coat round him and we walked as best we could until we could find a taxi.

'Where's Stephanie?' I whispered when we'd gone a little way. He told me they'd had a fight; that much was obvious. It wasn't the first time, but it'd been getting worse and this time they'd been drinking the whole weekend. He couldn't remember what started it. It seemed unbelievable to him, unreal. He shrugged – somehow he'd got one of her shoes

179

in his hand and then, extraordinary thing, he'd stabbed her in the eye with the heel, quick as if he'd swatted a fly. He'd wanted to. It hadn't just happened. When he'd grabbed a handful of her hair and jerked her head back, he had known what he would do. He slammed the spike in, but then he was so horrified at what he'd done, he ran. Toby ran away, he ran all the way to the Tate building and when the tide went out far enough, he made his confession in the sand. Toby had already called 999 and told them about Stephanie. He'd heard her as he ran down the stairwell, screaming obscenities at the top of her voice, so he thought she would live.

The taxi driver didn't want to take us. It was eleven in the morning and Toby smelled like a tramp had spat him out. I smiled my best smile and paid what the driver asked for up front. He let us get in.

'There'd better not be any trouble. Just 'ad it cleaned.'

I promised we'd be careful.

'I need to tell you something,' said Toby.

'It's OK, Toby. It's gonna be alright.'

'No, it isn't.'

'Shh.'

'No – about Sal.'

'What?' I didn't know how much more I could take. 'What about Sal? Fuck's sake Toby'

'It was the E. She took bad E.'

'What?'

My hand was raised and shaking. I don't know how I didn't slap him.

'No – that's not right.'

'I know, Gina listen…'

'She didn't do that! Not anymore.'

'She did, babe. She did a lot of things… Sorry.'

'No – I would've known.'

'Sorry G.'

180

'No. That's not right. The report – the tox report didn't say that.'

'Look, I'll be gone.'

'Too fucking right.'

'I hate it that you don't know.'

'Tell me then.'

'JTB paid for it.' His breathe escaped between his lips.

'John?'

'Yeah. And he paid me to keep my mouth shut.'

'What?' I couldn't understand what he was saying.

'G – *I* got them the stuff. It was *me*.' He hit his chest. 'It was me.' Then he bent forward and wept. I was so angry I couldn't speak. Angry with him. With John. All of it. E! I thought all that was in the past. I still didn't get it.

I rubbed his back, as he put his head on his knees. Then I jammed the back of his head with the palm of my hand, hard. I heard his nose crack as he yelled and tried to cover his face.

'Oi!' snapped a voice over the intercom.

'We're all right. No mess.'

Toby was waving his arms, fending me off. I slammed my heel into his foot.

'What about the tox report?' I was shouting. I wanted to hurt him more. 'There was a whole bunch of other stuff she'd taken, cough medicine, paracetamols. No E. '

'John. It was John.' Toby held his nose and tipped his head back. 'He wanted her to have a load on that night. He gave her the lot I reckon. She was up for it, G.'

'You tosser!' I said. Something was tapping the back of my brain, as if I had a question to ask but I ignored it, I just wanted to hurt Toby more.

'We're here. There'd better not be any muck back there,' said the driver.

We got out onto Borough High Street in bright sunshine. I tipped the cabby a couple more quid and took Toby into the station. It was empty apart from us and the desk sergeant, if that's what he was. When they'd finished with me, I called Elvis and then I called the Museum and took the day off, my stomach churning, my mind full of my sister. They were separated. He shouldn't have been anywhere near her or Bunyan Court that night. O Sal. She had given up taking all that crap. I knew she had. Everything shit in her life came from him.

II: Styx and Stones

Sal knows I am angry with her. She is whining.

'Everything is black and white to you. One thing or the other. *Little* sister.'

'Oh, shut up. You never know anything about anything,' I say. 'Deliberately vague.'

Sal is a door slammer, a vase thrower, so I wait – but nothing happens.

'Head in the sand' I say, pushing it just a bit. I won't be diverted by her tactics. Eventually she speaks again, still whining.

'I'm worried, Gina – I'm worried about Zoe'

'I know baby.'

'My *daughter*. My girl. You don't know what that's like. You've never had kids. Not of your own.'

I deal the cards again. I realise I am sucking my teeth, it is the only noise. I consider the layout and light a cigarette, dealing again. I look at Sal

'So, what do *you* think is going on?' I ask.

'Yeah, like *I* know,' she says. '*I* don't know anything anymore, do I?' Then she says – 'I'm just worried that Zoe's not around, you know?'

'I know,' I say. 'Me too.'

She is close now, whispering in my ear – 'I know what it looks like. Maybe.'

'Yeah, well, what it looks like is what it is,' I say, flicking ash into a saucer.

'Never use an ashtray, do you?'

In a few minutes I get out a different set of cards out, a vintage Cuban pack Sal bought for me once when she was on holiday. She watches.

'Those the Cuban ones? You haven't used these ones before, have you?'

I tell her they don't like me to touch them, but they feel right today.

I try a different configuration, a circle, don't like what I see.

Then, I am done. I've made up my mind.

I know Sal is uncomfortable. She starts gabbing just to fill the space.

'My little sister, Gina. Always been sensible. *So* strong. Don't know where you get it from because Mum's limp as loose elastic. Dad wasn't what you'd call reliable and it's true what you say Gina, that I'm evasive. Sorry about that, I know you're right. You're always sorting things out for people, aren't you? Dealing with the shit. And, you know what, you still surprise me – take this Tarot thing. It was Ouija when we were kids, you remember?'

I say, 'Of course. I've still got the board you painted for me, the one with me in the middle as a witch queen, all in white. It's at Bunyan Court, in the sideboard where John keeps his whisky.'

'We did Ouija all the time when we shared a room, didn't we? But then we stopped and neither of us did it anymore for some reason. Found boys or something, probably. Still, you've got the Tarot now.'

'Shall we have another look then,' I say although I can sense her reluctance. She goes off on a tangent again having a go at me, but I let her speak.

'How's the job, Gina? Still some sort of museum clerk? Boring desk job, anyway.'

I smile. Flick ash into the saucer. I know this game.

'Still wearing that ugly suit? It makes your calves look big. No scarf, no earrings, no colour at all, you should get your colours done G.'

'I will,' I say.

'Does everyone in a Miss Accomplished suit do the Tarot then? All that front you put on, are they all at it?'

'Only me,' I say, and wait.

'How are we going to make her talk to us then?' She asks me the next time. 'I need you to sort this thing with Zoe for me. I mean, what can *I* do?'

I'm sitting at the kitchen table looking at three Tarot packs, which I have not yet dealt.

'Haven't you got any ideas?'

'Like what...'

'What do you want to happen here, Sal?' I tap my forefinger on the cards.

'Don't you ever give a straight answer?'

'Do you *always* have to have the last word?'

We laugh and she follows me over to the kettle; I make some tea and stare at my reflection in the window, hoping to see Sal at my shoulder. She wants me to deal for her, for Zoe – and I will, when she asks me to.

'You've been watching?' Sal asks.

'I've been watching,'

'Who?'

'I watch all of you. Zoe, and mum, and you.'

It seems like she knows this, but at the same time, she's confused. 'How *long* have you been watching us?'

'Always. Ever since – since it's been – necessary.'

'How do you, you know, watch?'

I deal the cards, a standard Rider-Waite set I tell her, because they are the easiest.

I place a photo on the table. Zoe is in my arms at her christening.

'Who took this?' Sal asks. 'Where's everybody else? Where's the cake?'

I concentrate on the photo and deal again.

'Colourful, aren't they? Interesting.'

'Can you feel their pull?' I ask, although I know she can.

'What's this one?' she says.

'In a minute.'

'Why is that one turned over?'

'In a minute.'

'I think she's OK. You think she's OK, don't you Gina?'

'In a minute.'

'Right – here we go,' I say. 'Let's talk. About Zoe.'

I have the cards laid out and I touch them in a particular order, which is like touching your navel or places on your face, I tell her – you feel the place even before you touch it.

'Yes,' she says.

'I don't see her as hurting too much, Sal. It's not like that.'

'So she's not suffering,' Sal whispers.

'I think I could tell if she was in trouble. Or in pain.' I make my voice strong, confident.

'Not in pain.'

'I don't think she's unhappy either, as such.'

'Not unhappy.' She thinks about that. 'What does it mean?'

'So, it's like – she's been on a binge somewhere. Out of it. Out of touch.'

'For two months? Really?'

'Something like that,' I tell her.

'I don't get it.'

'OK Sal – it's like she's sleeping. Out of it, right.'

'Maybe.'

'She might wake up any time. When she wakes up, she's going to – like, call you. Or me, if she can't get through to you. If I'm the one who's – nearest.'

'Alright,' she says.

'Nobody knows when she'll wake up Sal, or what she'll do then.'

'Yeah. She'll let us know. When she can, maybe?'

'I think so.'

The bright colours of the cards flash across the table, then I sweep them away again. Soon they are back in lines, flowing in a direction that I can feel although nothing is visible. I hope she can feel it now too. Using the cards is like entering a stream or a river, I tell her, the water is telling us to lie down and allow the current to carry you where you need to go. Sal starts to mumble, talking to herself: My daughter. My girl. Travelling. No word. It's not like her. It frightens me and I don't think I can handle this. I can't.'

'Calm down. Calm *down,* Sal.'

'Why can't I speak to her?'

'It's like Mum,' I say. 'Before Mum – moved closer. It's going to be alright. You'll work it out, Sal. You will.'

'Yeah, well mum talks to me now. We're getting on fine now.'

'I know, sweetie. I know.'

I let it go for a few days then start up again, trying to get Sal to understand what I need her to know.

'Something on your mind, little sis,' she says. 'You don't give up, do you?'

'No, I say. Come on.' I get the cards out again. 'Here we go, Sal. Let's do one for you.'

The cards I try this time are different – she hasn't seen these before. They're artistic. Colourful, but controlled; the pictures are not wild art, if you know what I mean. All Tarot are beautiful in their way, but these have a wistful quality.

'Concentrate now,' I say. 'These are the *Tarot del Dulce Crepusculo*. Sweet and sad.' I show them to her, before I lay them out. There is one card Sal doesn't like. It has facemasks with orange hair and white spaces where there should be eyes. The eyes have floated away from the masks and drifted into a line along the middle of the card, sitting in flowing water, like a river of eyes where you don't know which masks are the original ones above and which are the reflection in the water. It troubles her.

'What side of the river are we on?' she says. 'I want to say, to know, which side of the river I am on, but I can't decide.'

'Don't let it worry you,' my voice is as soothing and offhand as I can make it.

I flick through the pack and choose certain cards.

'Now you read,' I tell her.

'I don't read Tarot.'

'Read the pictures. Just look at the pictures and let's see what they tell you.'

I have selected three cards. She finds the artwork engaging.

'They're like individual vignettes, stunning really. I'd have done them differently though. If I have the energy, I might make you a Tarot deck one day, when I've got nothing on.'

'C'mon,' I say. 'Describe them.'

The first one is XXI – *Il Mundo* – a huge face like a Manga fairy set in the globe of the world, beautiful, turquoise; she weeps her loss in a river of silver tears - it flows into a wide bowl held high by a priestess, standing on a lunar volcano.

'So the world has lost something,' she says. 'And it's sad.'

I nod. 'That's right, in a way. Something has come to an end, been completed.'

'I see. Is it about a person then?'

I nod again. I push another card forward on the table:

XIX – *Il Sole*– three faces, angelic, wisps of hair covering their features, all facing different directions as three Janus facets of a benign sunset in the sky.

'So there are three girl spirits – is it spirits?'

'It's you reading, so it's what you see in the card.'

'OK. So, they look kind of similar, don't they? Like the same woman at different stages of her life.'

'Go on.'

'So like – mother, daughter, and what – grandmother?'

'That's it.'

It takes her a while. Then she is shocked, but not quite shocked. 'Wait a minute,' she says. Then: 'You bloody know-it-all bitch.'

Then comes the tantrum. Doors, vases, windows. I know the drill.

Now she's shouting:

'Oh you're so fucking wise, frog face!' Slam. 'You think you know everything! Well, you don't.' Crash of teapot falling to the floor. 'Don't know how to eat properly for a start. If it doesn't come on toast, you can't eat it.'

Actually those are my mother's words, more or less true.

I am not fazed; I push the third card towards her.

'Is this going on all night?' she shouts, but she looks at the card anyway.

VII – *Coppe* – there is a sad girl, long dark hair; she sits by a riverbank looking deep into the water. An elegant skeleton wearing a long black evening dress, also with long dark hair looks back at her, not from the surface, but from within the river, perhaps lying on the river bed, perhaps inside the water.

Quietly, Sal speaks. 'They are smiling at each other, these girls; they are reflections of each other aren't they? – but – they can never touch, can they? Not anymore, and that's how it has to be.'

III: Cuckmere Haven

It was September when Elvis and I drove down to the coast for a day of fresh air and some outdoor swimming on his part. It was near Lewes where our first stop was, which according to him is a town for people who can't hack Brighton anymore and tell themselves they can be anywhere they want to be inside an hour, which is true if all you're talking about is Gatwick airport. The name is *Lew-iss,* but Elvis kept calling it *Loos.* That rhymes with the River Ouse, which he pronounced *Owss,* proving he wasn't a local boy, or maybe just to annoy me. The river noses silently through the middle of the town, a body of water notable mostly in connection with Virginia Woolf. Elvis was headed for Barcombe Mills, which is a long stretch of the Ouse where people like to swim, challenging their immune system the old-fashioned way by exposure to dangerous pathogens. It was called 'wild swimming', which Elvis usually did at Hampstead. I stayed in the car. I had brought Wuthering Heights on the Kindle.

Eventually Elvis had arfed around with enough like-minded nutters to want a hot cup of tea, so I got the small picnic basket and thermos out of the boot and put down a blanket smelling of something that had barely survived previous picnics, or shouldn't have.

'Is it always this hot down here?' he asked, licking cream off his fingers.

'No,' I said. 'Sometimes, it's windy.'

'Fair enough. Pass the jam. Please.'

'Oh, everything's such a fucking mess Elvis. I don't know where to start,' I said.

'Oh right, don't bottle it up then. Let's have it.' He pulled on a jumper and leaned against the wheel of his red Cinquecento, blocking it out with his bulk. I had a packet of cigarettes in my bag but I daren't get them out, I'd never hear the end of it after how long it had taken me to give up,

189

and the weight I was still battling. He'd make the whole day about that. Or maybe he wouldn't – he knew me to well.

The thing was, now it came to it, I didn't know how to get the words out. That thing they say – you feel like climbing the walls – I felt like that, like a rat trying to scrabble out of a box and always falling back in. I had felt like that since I had taken Toby to Borough Police Station. And I couldn't sleep.

'JTB,' said Elvis. 'What's going on with him just now?'

'Same.'

The words just didn't come. I wanted to talk but I had so much anger about JTB I didn't know where to start. I leaned against Elvis and he chewed a long stem of grass, holding my hand.

'I'm supposed to call him. About Zoe.'

'When?'

'Well I haven't made an appointment…'

'Do it now.'

'I've been calling him a lot – he's sick of me nagging, he gets angry.'

'Course. You're putting him under pressure.'

'Then he's nasty.'

'He knows he's a crap dad.'

'Yeah, well, everybody knows that.'

'Perhaps he thinks you're going to call his mother again.'

'Do you think I should?'

'No – call him.'

I sipped my tea and then I called JTB. He turned off his phone when he saw who was calling, but I have all his numbers and I got him in the end. 'What are you doing about Zoe?' I asked him. 'If you won't try to find her, I will go,' is what I said. 'And I'll send you the bill.' I would have as well, only I'd have sent them to his mother first. Maybe he suspected that.

I thought Elvis probably heard most of what JTB said, but I told him about it anyway.

190

'I think he's worried I'd go and see him if he hadn't got moving.'

'Too right. So what's happened?'

'He used the 'c' word twice.'

'Tosser. What did he say?'

'The detective's found her – he's been looking since he got all my calls, he just didn't want to tell me.'

'Oh that's so great – what's she doing?'

She's in Brazil…in a…'

'What happened to Argentina? I thought she was in …'

'She's in a hospital.'

'Oh my God – what's happened?'

'She's got a broken neck.'

'What the fuck…'

'I know. She fell out of a window they think – in this place, a favela thing that's supposed to have been cleaned up.'

'Sanitised. Pacified. Something …'

'Santa Marta. Her face is bad.'

'How – bad?'

'Don't know.'

''And they've kept her drugged.'

'What, like in a coma?'

'I don't know. I think so.'

He pulled at the grass, shredding the seed heads and chucking them towards the water

'Oh, but they'll bring her back now, surely?'

'Transfer back to London was inadvisable apparently, *yada yada yada*. Anyhow, JTB's bringing the full force of his personality to bear on the insurance company, so...'

'Is he really not going to Rio?'

'Apparently not. I'll go, I told him. It's his daughter. Bastard.'

'Just when you think he can't get worse.'

'I want to go and get her, but it'll cost a shit load, I'll have to take unpaid holiday – which they don't like, and she could be back home before I get there if he sorts all that out.'

'What you going to do then?'

'I want – I want him dead.' The words were out. They didn't surprise me as much as thought they would.

'Oh, f' god's sake,' Elvis rolled his eyes.

'No, honestly. I do. I think about it all the time. I think about doing it all these different ways.'

'Oh, p-lease!'

'I think about stabbing him.'

'With what?'

'A kitchen knife.'

'As if...'

'I'll do it one day. Really.'

'Fuck's sake.'

'Well fuck you.'

'And you ... OMG, Gina Greenshaw – *What* has got into you?'

'He's such a fuck. I can smell him in the flat. I can't stand it.'

'Alright now.'

I couldn't hold back the sobs. 'He's taken over, and it's like she was hardly there – but it's where she died.'

Elvis rubbed my back. 'Alright lovely, it's alright.'

We got back in the Cinquecento, me lying scrunched on the tiny shelf that was supposed to be the back seat. If I complained about the space, he would tell me to ask Santa for driving lessons. We were going to Cuckmere Haven next for a walk, a place of meadows, cliffs and shingle beach that I knew well. I had spent a weekend there doing my Duke of Edinburgh camping in the sixth form, in the days when they let you camp by the river. It's all protected there now, but I think you can still swim in the meanders, which are cut off from the main river and have no tide. Elvis will know. You can definitely swim in the sea, which is only a couple of miles from the car park, and the pub – the Golden Galleon at Seaford, site of many an underage drinking binge in my youth. Strange to think Sal and I will never go there again, never show our kids our old haunts. Not that I've got any kids.

We didn't go down to the beach. I wanted to do the South Downs Way path up over the cliff tops and look out to sea. It was windy when we got there and the sea was rough; the tide was coming in, bringing a smear of damp with it as seagulls tried to ride the thermals and screamed at us to go home. It can be peaceful there but I liked the bluster and the cold that day. I think perhaps I thought we'd talk some more about the JTB thing then, but we couldn't hear each other so I gave up trying and we trudged on, heads into the wind. It was getting dark by the time we made it to the Golden Galleon, over the bridge and up the steps and everything was coming back to me. Elvis got the drinks in and I asked for a 'purple nasty' just to see what he'd do. He got me one. I don't know if the pub served them, or if Elvis had known what it was; I didn't ask.

A purple nasty is cider and beer with cassis in it. It's curdled and it tastes horrible but it makes you drunk and then it makes you sick, which is the point. The rain started up properly, beating against the picture window behind my seat. They had a fire going in the grate and a barman came to put more logs on it, which perked me up a bit. I started to talk about JTB.

I talked about how I lay in bed thinking of all the ways I wanted to kill him. How I couldn't stick the fact that he won every game, every time. I knew how it would feel to push a kitchen knife between his ribs and watch raspberry foam bubble on his lips. I could see the pieces of his skull sticking to the carpet after I'd hit him with Sal's *Big Bertha* – a golf club shaped like half a loaf of bread. I could see in his eyes that Elvis thought I was drunk. Unravelling. I had lived with these thoughts for more than a year and the frustration never went away. Now there was Zoe – Zoe was the important thing. I had promised Sal I would find her and look after her and now it looked like JTB was going to stop me doing that as well, but at least he'd found her. I didn't know how he always neutralised me so easily. I didn't tell Elvis that I lie awake and speak to Sal. I hadn't lost it completely.

IV: Bunyan Court

JTB used 208 Bunyan Court to meet his women. Sal had even known that although she didn't talk about it. His presence was one of the reasons I didn't go back there much – it was like den that had been sprayed by a male fox and I could smell semen and his aftershave in every room.

If I'd been stronger, if I had stood up to him more – he would have maybe fucked off somewhere else and Sal wouldn't be dead.

I spent some time thinking about that flat. It was near to work and I'd had enough of paying rent to live in Clapham. Ned, the reason I moved there, had left two years into our relationship and because JTB was all over Bunyan Court I hadn't made it back, but the flat was half mine, morally it was all mine and I had decided I wanted to go back there now; it's in the Barbican, this remnant of 1970s greyness frozen in concrete, a Brutalist ziggurat in the City of London. Our flat didn't even overlook the lakes and hanging gardens you suddenly came across, just when you thought you were lost in a 1930's tenement block. We overlooked the YMCA and a building site, but everybody gets one of those in London. On the positive side, we had our own orchestra, a kick-ass cinema and top class modern dance on demand, all the more elitist for the infrequent advertising and lack of useful signage. Even a resident could be on her way to the toilets and find she had run out of orange carpet, only to miss the whole performance trying to find her way back, wandering in a panic through remote stairways and unexpected levels of the car park.

I could walk to work – the Museum of London was on the same estate but I had tubed it in from Clapham every day because I couldn't stand the thought of coming in at night and finding JTB shagging someone else in that flat, especially after what he'd done to Sal. Because their divorce hadn't gone through before Sal died, he owned her half now, and he didn't want to sell. He wanted my half. He could have bought any flat in London and much better ones than the arse end of the Barbican, but he was just being nasty for a change, trying to control everything – he didn't even work in the City anymore, barrow boy come good that he was, just like my father. I thought I would strangle him; throw the kitchen knives at him, gas him with the fire extinguisher if I found him in bed with some young thing who didn't know what he was like. So mostly I had stayed away.

A lot of my stuff was still there so I didn't have to bring much – after all the trepidation, I moved back in, just like that. Looking round the flat, which really was not much more than a couple of matchboxes and a bathroom smaller than you get on an airplane, JTB hadn't changed anything. I had somehow imagined a round red velvet bed worthy of *Shaft* and all my stuff in the hall, but nothing had changed and, bless his cotton boxers, it was still there, my very favourite photo in the world. It was huge, a photo of Sal and me as kids together, which my dad had taken. I got it enlarged on canvas and hung it above the sofa so you saw it when you walked in the flat. We were on Brighton beach, heads touching, grinning gap-toothed grins at the camera, looking naughty; the tide was out, and our hair blew behind us in mingled ratty beach hair, which is what my mother used to call 'rat-tails and ribbons'.

The first night there I tried to get Elvis to come round but he wasn't picking up. I found six bottles of champagne and bottle of scarlet nail polish and some out of date Benecol in the fridge so I sat and painted my toenails. I looked at that picture and had a drink or two alone, listening to my old LPs, starting with Year of the Cat. She was the pretty one, Sal, I had always known that, with a smile that made you laugh even in a photo. But with all that charm she had been stupid as well, and unlucky, and I wasn't really sure when I noticed the signs. Too late, anyway. We lived together for nearly three years, until Sal got pregnant with Zoe and moved in with JTB, thrilled to bits to have bagged a big cheese. Was that the beginning of the downward slope? It must have been seeded earlier than that. She had always smoked weed – but was there much other stuff going on back then as well? It was even possible that she'd been madly in love, she must have been because JTB was such a wanker than in her right mind even Sal would have noticed that. She must have been off her face for years.

Once JTB began to show his colours she used to come to Bunyan Court to get some space, and maybe to see me for a bit. He never hit her or anything, not that I know anyway, but he was *so* controlling, *so* unforgiving of any weakness that she would be shaking when she put the key in her front door. This little flat was ours, from our dad and one of the few things that we had kept from closer times and I knew Sal had felt safe there which made what happened to her seem so much worse.

Zoe used to come round a lot as well, because her school was close by and I didn't mind if she hung out here. They both kept a few clothes and toiletries in the flat and I liked that because I felt connected to them, like they might come and stay any time. One of them must have let JTB copy her key but they never admitted it – they both knew I wouldn't want him anywhere near, which is probably why the bastard used Sal's room for his sexual incontinence later. Or maybe my irritation simply hadn't registered with him. Who knew why he did anything?

It was around then that Toby got in touch, when I was settling back in. There was a message on my phone from someone I didn't know, saying Toby couldn't email and wanted to know if it was alright to talk. I should ring Wandsworth Prison and set up a visit. I didn't want to visit him. I had no wish to go to a prison and get felt up by the guards and have my mobile nicked by one of the visitors' kids, but I knew I was going to have to do it. I'd looked in the Tarot and there she was as I had known she would be – Temperance, the bridge between the past and the future, the conscious and unconscious. Toby still had things to tell me. I knew I might never have the complete picture of the night Sal died. I had a much better idea once Toby got going. He had wanted to tell me about it forever and now he had the chance, he couldn't shut up.

'Well, after she was with JTB, she was one of my biggest clients, G.'

I didn't even want to look at him. He was clean, hair parted and brushed, he looked like someone else.

'I don't get it,' I said.

'Yeah, E mostly. She told me she liked him when she was on it. And he liked her when she was on it, stands to reason. He didn't touch it.'

'Yuk!'

'The love drug you know.'

'Don't tell me.'

'They used to party at Bunyan Court, get away from home with it you know.'

'They had room at home – their house is huge.'

'Not the same though, is it?'

They came and got out of it and sometimes I'd be there, hiding in my room pretending not to hear them party. I should have taken up the tuba or something, a big instrument that I could have practised and drowned out their noise only I had more respect for our neighbours than that. I guess I had known some things, I used to kid myself she didn't know I was there but she did. She behaved badly to a lot of people in those years; I didn't want to talk to Toby about any of this.

Over time Sal got worse. Not fast – at first you couldn't tell unless you knew her. They had a nanny-housekeeper person called Jo who liked Sal and covered for her, so life just went on round her. She got away with it for years, being disconnected but just managing to keep things together. Then came the summer where they didn't have Jo anymore. The kids were home for the holidays and Sal hardly got out of bed for the whole of July. JTB had a lot of 'business trips' at that time, so after the first week of calls from Zoe and complaints from Peter about the food, I grudgingly moved in with them for a while to help out as best I could in between work and whatever else had seemed important at the time. JTB was as thrilled as I was.

He would come in the door and try to see if I was in their basement kitchen while he hung his keys up and took his shoes off in the hall. He did this thing where he leaned over the bannister to listen downstairs whilst squinting up the stairwell in case I was up there, and loosening his tie at the same time. He never got it right and I could always see him in the hall mirror anyway. I ignored him, carried on reading the newspaper or whatever but when he found me, he wouldn't say hello, he'd flick his grey forelock, look at his silk socks and ask me what there was to eat. Oh, Gina – er, what's there to eat? He didn't exactly have lipstick on his collar but he may as well have. He didn't ask if the kids were in or how Sal had been today. In retrospect, I could have been more polite, although I didn't feel like it at the time. It was the same every night, I did it to wind him up –

I opened the big door of their American fridge, took out some milk and passed him the Asda cornflakes, which I bought specially for him because he liked designer granola. He got a beer and left. I never saw him eat at home unless his mother was there, he even had breakfast at the gym. The rest of the time he was out, or listening to his German sound system on his fancy headphones.

'Your mother had depression didn't she?' Toby said.

None of his fucking business, but I knew what he was getting at.

'Sal told me once,' he continued. 'It was worse for her though, going cold turkey at the same time and that.'

It should have been obvious but I didn't see it. JTB knew. There'd been years of parties and clubbing and never coming down so people had come to think all that manic running around was normal bubbly Sal. Even me.

'Didn't see it, did I?' I said. 'Don't know why. Shit.'

'We both didn't do her justice, did we?' He reached for my hand across the table but I pulled back.

'What about your other clients Toby?' I was beginning to shout. He stood up to go.

'She lost the eye you know! Did you know that? Steph lost her eye.'

I thought he'd crumple. He didn't.

'She loves me. You don't get it. She's waiting for me.'

It was me who crumpled. I hoped it wasn't true. Was I off kilter with the whole bloody world?

When Sal had begun to recover, would talk a bit, I made her see people – doctors, a counsellor, her hairdresser. She wouldn't see friends. The kids did whatever they did, even I didn't watch out for them properly although I told them off a lot; it was all the parenting I knew how to do. They call it 'middle class neglect'. It's when people get so involved in their careers, their divorces and their own problems that they don't notice their kids losing their virginity behind a tree somewhere or passing out drunk on the circle line on a school night. Finally, JTB's mother came down one weekend and performed a miracle. She actually slapped John.

I had made a pathetic attempt at a Sunday roast. They gravy was solid and the veg were wet and cold by the time I got the chicken to the table, but Mrs ate it stoically and asked me about the children, who weren't there and nor was John although we'd laid places for them. Sal sat smiling out of the window, pretending to eat. We got on well, Mrs and I. She knew we were struggling and she didn't blame me, although I think I could have done better looking back on it. She was like Barbara Windsor with posh vowels, her eyes were alive and she'd had her teeth done, amongst other things if you knew what you were looking for. According to Sal, the vowels had arrived when JTB got his first serious bonus.

When John turned up, around four o'clock, he was pissed and she let him have it in front of us. She was like Boudicca in tweed and JTB was crushed for once.

'Listen, Mum, it's not like you think,' hand to his sore cheek.

Yes it was, she knew it was, she knew her son.

He was shocked, not that she hadn't hit him before, but now she'd done it in front of us. Sal had to pay for it later, but the upshot was that Peter went to a posh boarding school where they fed him and made sure he turned up for classes and Zoe, who was as stubborn as her gran, wouldn't go to boarding school or move in with Mrs no matter what, got three GCSEs instead of about eight and never told anybody where she was. She wouldn't text and she wouldn't answer her phone.

Sal got a Labrador called CoCo and went for walks in Richmond Park, Hampstead Heath, Greenwich, places like that – I joined her when I could. JTB threw money at the problem and told her to get more help, and even though she tried for a while, Sal was left with a dodgy heart and a darkness that never really went away. I thought she settled down but I couldn't get inside her head. I knew she was only making the expected noises, she wasn't talking to me; not really. The shadows had only receded toward the edges, like peripheral vision, threatening to crowd in on her at any time. She kept it all to herself.

John hardly missed a beat through all of this – just that one brilliant moment when his mother's diamond hand connected with his cheek. Other than that, he was having a great time running around with endless other women and getting promoted at his investment company. He was flying.

In the end, Sal kicked John out a year before she died and made a weak stab at getting divorce proceedings off the ground – for which I harangued her and tried to goad her to be more aggressive; her lawyer was a drip and nobody seemed able to find out how much JTB was worth; he seemed to have dodgy lawyers on speed dial, they came out of the woodwork so fast. The thing was, contrary to what she let me believe, Sal had never stopped seeing him. Did I know? I don't think so. Toby had known about that, so had Zoe – maybe everybody knew except me. No-one told me and I believed what she said. I could have helped. I didn't need to be in Clapham by then – I would have moved back and we could have lived in Bunyan Court for nearly three years, despite JTB's nasty habits. What Zoe didn't know was how much they still met up and still had sex. He was doing it with everybody else in the world there, he may as well fuck his wife in her own flat.

'She used to look beautiful Gina – she always looked good, even then,' said Toby the last time I went to see him.

'When?'

'When she went to all those dos with him, like he made her go with him so he'd let her have the car and that.'

'What? What car?'

'C'mon Gina – you know what he's like.' Toby was looking nervous. Shifty. 'If she behaved, he would let her have the car. If she behaved, he would sign the documents. Only he never did.'

'No, he didn't.'

'She had to go to all the corporate dos with him, all dressed up so he looked good, stable and no trouble, and then he'd promise her something she wanted. If not, he was going to talk about her mental state in the divorce and she'd get nothing. Anyway, that's what he told her.'

'Fucker – I didn't know about this.'

'Yeah, she was all diamonds and nails, high shoes an' her hair done by Harry again. She had to, but she liked it as well.'

'It was like, a kind of torture. Christ I hate him.'

'They used to go back to your flat and I'd bring them whatever she'd ordered.

'Jesus Toby.'

'I made a lot of money off them.'

They went back to the Barbican flat to talk and get high where the kids wouldn't find out what he was doing to her, although they were probably lost and out of it with their mates themselves by then. JTB didn't take anyone back to his own place – why would he when he had mine to shit in?

'What about that night Toby?'

'See, that's the thing I had to tell you Gina.'

'What happened? Tell me.' I pointed at him but he held my gaze. I'd heard part of the story already.

Toby supplied them that night, as always, although nobody else knew until he told me all about it in the taxi. John liked coke, may it choke him one day soon. What the hell was she thinking?

I guess she wasn't thinking at all.

'She had the blue sequined dress on, the one they showed at the inquest. It was for this charity thing they went to.'

'I know,' I said. I'd found it in the bathroom at Bunyan Court. She'd been seen in it earlier, out with JTB, but she hadn't been wearing it when she died. That blue dress was the colour of her eyes but I wasn't going to say that to Toby. I'm sure he knew anyway and didn't mention it either.

'I had a few drinks with them, they were sociable people G, and I gave her the stuff.'

'But you knew about her heart, didn't you?'

'G – I...'

'You did Toby. Oh yes you did. And the depression. You knew, and you gave her that crap anyway.'

'C'mon Gina. She'd have got it from somebody else. JTB would have made sure.'

'You...'

'JTB would have made sure she got her candy from somewhere. She wouldn't shag him without it.'

'They were supposed to be getting divorced.'

'Yeah, well, they were, but she still had to party with him when he wanted her to.'

'She didn't have to do that.'

'She thought she did. She hit the booze big time that night as well.'

'I know.' It was in the tox report.

JTB said it would be fine, he would look after her, and Toby, the tosser, he just did it. He gave her the stuff and pocketed the money. He thought she popped the lot and then sat with one Kir Royale after the other, listening to Toby talk about people she knew. Half an hour later she was going through the roof. She took her clothes off. I could hardly bear to hear about it.

'JTB thought it was hilarious. She was shouting and singing and trying to get JTB to do her right there in front of me, she wanted me to video it on my mobile.'

I groaned. I wanted to hear it but I didn't want to know.

'Thing was, JTB was laughing the whole time. It was weird; I don't know how much he knew. Anyway, she was burning hot and had, like, no inhibitions at all.'

I put my hand into my pocket and squeezed my nails into the palm. There had been nobody on her side, not even me.

'The funny thing was,' Toby said, 'there was a look in her eye, like she seemed to know what was happening, like she was watching herself from behind her own head, like a dream you know.' He looked at his hands. There was a new tattoo, barbed wire round his wrist; I hadn't known you could get tattoos done in prison.

'At one point Sal said she felt sick, but she couldn't bring anything up,' Toby told me. 'I was like, reasonably compos I guess, and I tried to get her to drink some water but she wouldn't have it. JTB wanted me to go. He said, I'm on it Tobz mate, no worries, you get off. So I did.'

Toby ducked when he said that, maybe he thought I was going to go for him again, and I might have in other circumstances, but we were being watched all the time; the relaxed visiting ambience was pure illusion.

'Look G, I'm not saying I wasn't worried, but be fair, she was with her husband. When I left, JTB was trying to get her into a dressing gown and had his mobile in his hand. I didn't know what they cut with.'

The toxicology report showed that Sal had taken a Paracetamol overdose, but that didn't kill her, it didn't get the chance. She had a large amount of alcohol in her system along with ephedrine, a herbal stimulant you get in diet pills and something called dextromethorphan which was a cough suppressant. I'd looked it all up, I thought she'd been taking those because she'd been feeling so shit all the time and I hadn't thought much about the volume they found. I should have looked that up. It's what they cut the E with – there was no MDMA in it.

I never understood the Paracetamol before. Toby said JTB must have shoved them down her throat but I was starting to think she had done it herself in the bathroom where they couldn't see. I think, she couldn't stand the thought of what she'd have to go through, to sort her life out again after she had backslid – because I now know that night wasn't the first in the recent spate; it must have been very dark for her and she didn't want to go that road again, couldn't face her children or anything else. So she made sure she'd check out, one way or the other. It was her heart that went, which was a good thing because when she hit the railing all that way below, she ruptured her liver and broke so many of her bones that the thought of her lying undiscovered in a pissy stairwell until half way through the next afternoon is more than I can bear.

JTB told Toby he put a T-shirt and knickers on her and left her on the sofa, lolling about drunk. I didn't even know they'd seen each other until the inquest. He said they'd parted on Pall Mall after the charity shin dig. His evidence was that he had put her in a taxi and sent her home to the kids – maybe they were even there, nobody checked on them. He went on to another do where people vouched for him till four in the morning. Some Australian slapper knew exactly where he went after that, because it was to her hotel room where they stayed till after breakfast the next morning. So, true to form, JTB left my sister, drunk and depressed, having put her in her pyjamas on the sofa, and went out to party and was capable of getting it up with somebody else a few hours later.

She died in Bunyan Court, and I hadn't known any of the crap she was going through. Why didn't she tell me? Not knowing why she'd killed herself, it killed me.

I met Elvis for a drink at the Dog when I got back. He didn't sound surprised either. I was shouting by the end when I told him what Toby said about JTB.

'So, you're going to kill him now, is that it?' he said.

'That's right.'

'Right.'

'You do realise it's not like I know *when* he left, do I? Did he see her jump? Did he help? Bastard.'

'But OK, let's say you have a go,'

'Too right.'

'Yeah OK, well let's say you get the chance right – could you really do it? I mean can you *do* it? Stick the knife right in and that.'

'Yes. Totally.'

'Let's say you don't quite, you know, finish him – that you, maybe, lose your nerve right at the last minute.'

'I wouldn't. I'd do it; I'd come up behind him with a baseball bat and take his fucking head off.'

'He'd sue you into the ground Gina, he'd get you so convicted that you'd never get out. You'd never work and never see the kids or anybody else – and all for what?'

'For my fucking sister, bitch!'

'For Sal, lovely Sal, who was a mess, yeah, and who isn't coming back.'

'Fuck you.'

'C'mon Gina. What about Zoe now.'

'Ach Christ.'

I got a text from Zoe one day a few weeks later; I was at work, making the tea in the staff kitchenette thing round the back of the loos. The text took me by surprise because I'd kind of got into a depression of sorts myself, only I don't do depression. Elvis hadn't been around much and I hadn't been going out, only to work, catching up with my Londinium Matron Blog and the cataloguing that never goes away. I had stopped planning, stopped seeing people, stopped talking to Sal, just stopped. People kept their distance, which was fine by me.

Hi Gina. Itsme. Cmg home. Cple days. Dad got tkt.

My first reaction was fury. So *Daddy's* bloody got his fucking act together has he? So now we're all grateful because *Daddy's* pulled his finger out at last. Well yippy do. I revisited all my daydreams of hitting him with a baseball bat and watching all his teeth and spit flying in a red arc up to the ceiling and of jabbing a paperknife under his ribs until his life bubbled through his nose.

'What the hell is this?' My colleague, Phil, held up a mug of hot water with a dash of milk, two sugars, but no tea bag.

'Sorry Phil. Hang on.'

Back in the kitchenette, I texted Elvis:

Help me.

?

Zoes owh!

Kk cu on thbridge @ lunc

Xx

Even from a distance I could see Elvis had lost weight. He stood in the middle of the bridge, opened his arms and enfolded me in his big coat and gave me a hug that felt so good I could have cried.

He had brought two of his famous egg and cress Subs for us and a couple of Lattes that were too hot and we hung over the grey water, eating and playing pooh sticks with bits of bread. As I laughed and began to relax for the first time in weeks, I took note of the changes I could see, and these were just the external ones. Elvis was always careful of his appearance but now the word was 'groomed'. He was closely shaven, his shirt was ironed and his hair was suspiciously short. I knew what that meant. I elbowed him in the ribs.

'You're back on the wigs, right?'

'Something like that.'

'Cagey…'

'Not really, but tell me about Zoe.'

And so I let it go, missed my opportunity to see the obvious. Preoccupied with Zoe, I filed the wigs for later investigation which was lucky because if I'd pushed, dragged it out of him, tried to claim him, things might have turned out differently. Worse differently.

'I've decided to stay at Bunyan Court,' I told him.

'Oh. That's nice. Don't change the subject.'

'I want Zoe to live with me. If she wants to.'

'What about JTB? He'd rather have her at home.'

'Too busy to look after her, I hope.'

'Maybe. He'll give up his shag flat just like that will he?' Elvis scrunched the sandwich papers into a ball and made as if to throw it into the water. I caught his arm.

'He has to. Or I'll tell his kids what he's like. I will.'

'Maybe.'

'What if she doesn't want to live with me?'

'No chance,' he said looking me right in the eye. 'She knows more about her dad than you think.'

'You don't know that.'

'Yeh, I do. Really – she's been around more than you think.'

'So what – she's not – they're all what – trying to protect me?'

'Course they are.'

'Fuck off.'

'We all are.'

Too much. Couldn't handle it. Tears and snot galore.

V: Damnation

'We're going to be late.'

'We've got *a-ges*.' Zoe's voice echoed from the bathroom. I could tell she was doing her eye makeup. This would take a while.

'C'mon,' I said, louder. I was packing up the things we had spread all over the coffee table, but I wanted her to think I was ready or she'd take even longer.

I dusted crumbs from the crease, glancing at the dragon queen picture of me that Sal had drawn so many years ago. I folded the old board away and put it in the sideboard but it took me a few moments to locate the planchette, which had fallen under the table. Snatching it up, I found I didn't want to put it down again; I enclosed it in my palm, feeling its smooth warm shape – a heart with a window in it. Made of unpolished olive wood, it retained the touch of everybody who had ever held it in their hand; like suede. I lifted the fish-eye window to my eye and looked at Sal in our beach photo. Her hair was streaming behind her in the bluster of our day on Brighton Beach and we were laughing. I could still feel the press of her cheek against mine, smell the brown seaweed in her hand that she would throw at me as soon as the photo was done. Looking at that photo, I found I could remember her laughter. I hoped she could too.

Rain threatened as we walked as fast as we could in our heels to the Millennium Bridge.

'Not rain! Just today, *per-lease.*' Zoe was nearly out of breath, still recovering from her accident. I stole a look at her face as she looked ahead, checking for uneven slabs lying in wait for the precarious shoes she wore. There was a short, deep scar near her eye, which was starting to fade. She had covered that up with foundation, but it was the rough skin on her cheek that even stage makeup couldn't conceal; the rough pitted texture of scar tissue made the side of her face look like herbs strewn liberally across a chicken breast, although the other one was smooth. She said she couldn't remember falling from the window, or even why she was in Santa Marta and nor can anyone else, so they tell me. When she's ready, I will use every penny of JTB's money to find a cosmetic surgeon who can help her.

People were pouring onto the streets all around us. We were jostled by seven-foot showgirls of every type, although the broad theme had been designated as Mermaids of the World. People hurried towards the river as fast as they could. Zoe and I were heading for the Samuel Pepys, a wine bar on the City side with a view of the bridge; the balcony had been reserved for a small number of us hangers on and significant others. We wanted to be in place before they started the music or allowed people onto the beaches to watch the show because the crush was expected to be something else. Nothing like this had ever taken place before and we were having a front row view.

Elvis was in there somewhere, checking wigs and ordering people into position with megaphones, part of a team now. Danny Boyle was busy elsewhere but this was going to give the opening of the Olympics a run for its money. They started up the music to get everybody into the mood; I had brought my dad's binoculars – I didn't want to miss a thing. I began to strafe the bridge, looking for the most important person of the evening, the inspiration for the show, although she wouldn't be heading up the singing. They had a top showgirl from San Francisco called Damnation for that. The rock was in place in the middle of the bridge, as yet unoccupied. Carnival headdresses began to arrive in position along the bridge. I could see people spacing the showgirls in the manner that health and safety had designated, which was the condition on which the show rested and worked out with the observers from the Guinness book of Records – an arm's length apart and six feet from the railing, lined back to back facing the river both ways. That way they would be able to do their can-can kicks and if anybody fell they wouldn't hurt themselves or anybody else. Nobody was going to drown although

210

looking at the shoes, there might be a new record for broken ankles.

The music got louder and faster and the lights came on. A small gay man had the microphone.

'Ladies and Gentlemen, girls and boys, welcome to the show – the greatest Tranny Show on earth! Please would you put your hands together and welcome the star of the show, the gorgeous, the delectable, the one and only – Miss Lulu Damnation – and her inspiration – the fabulous *Miss Lorelei!*'

To explosive applause Damnation came to the fore out of the crowd. She raised her arms encased in white sequined gloves and took a deep bow, raising her right arm to introduce Lorelei, who bowed, flicked her long hair and settled herself elegantly onto the top of her rock where she arranged the folds of her spangled green and turquoise dress to look like the tail of a mermaid and tucked her feet into the plaster casing of her stage tail fins. The music exploded and the entire bridge full of showgirls began to sing. I so hoped they were showing this in Wandsworth prison. I trained my binoculars on Lorelei's face – she wore a sequined turquoise eye patch for the occasion and I could see her cheeks were wet. Her perfect glossy lips formed the words everyone was singing:

'It's raining men – Hallelluiah.'